P9-BZS-978

To the Memory of Yaacov Zipper, 1900-1983

All at once the Baal Shem Tov begins to speak:

"The sorrow of birth is greater than the sorrow of all the days of creation, and the sorrow of a single day of creation is more cruel than the sorrow of death."

The listeners become stiller than still and sway like the wheat of the fields and hearken .

"The child in the mother's womb lies in darkness, sucking the mother's juices and when the time comes for it to descend to the world, the mother is in mortal danger and the child wails. It is fearful of the light of day, of the white glare, the days and nights of solitude, the days and nights of heavy toil. So the child is consoled with soft words, rocked to sleep with a niggun, until it learns to look directly into the eyes of others. Then there is joy in the house of the mother and father — but the child is sad: it does not know how to bless creation. And when it does learn the blessing, the child recalls what it was taught in the mother's womb and it wails once again: 'I do not want to depart from this world.'

"So they say to him: You have played your niggun to the end. Now take it once more to the beginning."

... The Baal Shem Tov looks about and sees Dovid with his pallid, gentle face, and he motions him to his side.

"Tell me Dovid, what do you do with a niggun that has ended?"

"I begin to sing it once again," Reb Dovid fearfully answers.

"And when you come to the end once more?"

"I repeat the first refrain..."

"That means," the Baal Shem Tov elaborates, "that it ends at the beginning, and the niggun continues unbroken. Which means that were it not for the niggun, the universe, God forbid, could not exist. So continue to sing the niggun!"

CONTENTS

Yaacov Zipper was born in the Polish town of Shebreshin in 1900. Following an intensive Chassidic education in the traditional cheder, Zipper became committed to the secularist philosophy of Yiddish culture and trained as a teacher and youth educator. In 1925, he emigrated to Canada where he took up the teaching post at the Yiddish secularist Jewish Peretz Schools, becoming Principal in 1928. Throughout his life, Zipper was an important figure in Canadian Jewish literary affairs and played a leadership role in the Jewish Public Library, the Poalei Zion, the Jewish National Writer's Alliance, the Jewish Writers' Association and the cultural affairs of the Canadian Jewish Congress.

Yaacov Zipper wrote continuously from 1923 until his death in 1983 in both Yiddish and Hebrew, both short stories and novels. The recognition of his standing by international Yiddish-speaking audiences culminated in the award of the MANGER PRIZE FOR YIDDISH LITERATURE presented by the President of the State of Israel in 1982.

THE FAR SIDE OF THE RIVER will now enable a new generation of English language readers to sample the unique talents of the genius of Yaacov Zipper.

AT HOME AGAIN

THE TOWN is ancient. Although it has been rebuilt time and again it is still ringed by the same river. After every conflagration and calamity a legacy persists for generations, a tale to be heard and contemplated for oneself and others. My shtetl Tishevitz is old, exceedingly old, far older than the oldest synagogue in the land and the chronicle of terror and affliction which she and her children have endured is greater and longer than the long bridges over her waters which flow down to the vast sea.

She is one of the nine original settlements of the ancient region. Chmelnitski the tyrant — may his name be blotted out — laid seige to her. More than once were her children and elders victims of the despot's outstretched hand. On the dunes beyond the city Reb Aharon Kossack and the stalwart ruffians from the leather-workers' street resisted the invading hordes. The red gravestone in the old cemetery commemorates their deed.

Close by lies the remains of one of the unrevealed saints who, in the instant following his detection, departed the world one Friday evening in autumn. He was a mender of old clothes — a latutnik — who lived on the hill close to our home. For how big was all of Tishevitz? Everything was nearby. How distant am I from my grandfathers who actually had known the mender? My grandfathers knew him yet did not know his true identity. They brought him their threadbare clothing for patching and paid him with a three-pence coin and a Polish groshen. I look at my own coat, cut down from my older brother's kaputta, itself a remnant of an aged garment: Who knows, perhaps his touch, his glance, still lingers.

That is what I heard and thought about back home. I am certain that I was not alone in this. In many Jewish towns such

11

"menders" moved silently about, walking close by the walls, expiring in great anguish before candle-lighting time. In many Jewish homes children shuddered and quaked in the ink-black night of the bleak autumn. Who knows, perhaps along with the slanting rain the faint footsteps of the Messiah's precursor can be heard? Who knows, perhaps if we were able to discover the exact moment of assignation then each and every one of us might be found worthy? Who knows, perhaps he is already amongst us? So let us listen attentively to the tale grandmother tells and what the oil lamp reveals through its dark flickering flame. Perhaps we will hear it. Did not Reb Yechezkiel, the tax-collector of the Chassidic court, himself recount how it had been revealed to the Baal Shem Tov that when the true moment arrives, all would hear? Perhaps that moment is close at hand. Why do we not make ready?

* * *

For seven hundred years my town has been telling tales to my Hutchve River and, in turn, listens to the Hutchve's stories about the Viepcha, the Bug, the Son, and the remote distant aunt of them all, the Vysel.

We would play by the banks of the Hutchve, throw pebbles at her and tear pieces out of the earthen bridge that spanned her. Sometimes too, in the spring of the year, we dropped a cat into her waters, though — as God is my witness — our only wish was to guard the Hutchve from sinning, to prevent her from taking — God forbid — a human life. For did not everyone know that "He who takes the life of a living soul of Israel, it is as if he had destroyed a whole world?" How could we expose our Hutchve to that risk? She had to be provided with a scapegoat or else she might perish in the great heat, cease her murmuring, no longer listen to the story of her town, or reveal the secrets of the flotsam on the waters of the great land of Poland, refuge of the children of Israel to the day of redemption.

So for her sake we performed our deeds. And once again we heard the breaking of the waves and we mirrored ourselves in her waters where on moonlit nights the water-creatures emerged, those who know all the secrets of the watery deep and of the earth but who still yearn for human companions. By day the water-creatures are fearful of emerging; they want no one to see that their hands are really nothing more than folded down-feathers. They emerge from the waters by nightfall and wander about the shore until the young folk cross the Long Bridge to promenade in the countryside. Then the water-creatures steal along the waters, glide silently on the waves and merge with the young people, joining in their song, whispering secret tales.

* * *

Each time the Hutchve brings new evil tidings a cry is soon carried from the Vuhl to the hill where the "mender" lived on the Shule street, and yet further to Reb Aharon Kossack's tombstone. The red sands of the Kutchira dunes seem to respond: "We have heard those cries before, many times before; what is it to us that the evil-doers are here again." And fresh clods of red sand crumble into the open graves.

The cry exhausts itself, the weeping is drained of tears. For nights without end the Hutchve reflects the burning town — and once more tells a story. To every generation she recites the events anew, and every generation listens, endures, and contemplates the occurrence.

Sometimes, it happens that the waters carry one of her children into the distant world and when from afar he hears her murmuring voice, he longs for home. Oh how he pines, how silent he becomes. For who would listen and who would trouble to understand how a man who walks about in the tumult of alien streets actually sees before him the familiar narrow paths and fresh, yellow sand. Who would conceive that during an ordinary day, amidst the bustling din of the town square a man actually sees himself lying prone on a meadow, deep in the grasses, hearing once again the old water wheel splashing in the familiar waters. What does this man do? — he begins to tell himself a story.

And if no one is near he begins to sing a niggun. All at once the shadows lift from his eyes and he hears and sees and feels the earth beneath his feet and the sky above his head: home! His niggun is heard in the new land; it wanders over newly broken paths, quivering and fluttering there. *Is anyone listening? Does anyone see?*

So, once again, he tells himself the story. And like the peasant who plows deeply into the earth, he believes that the blessings of heaven and the moisture of the earth will descend upon it and someday a rich field of corn will flourish along the shores where his child lies by the river banks listening to the rustling stalks, absorbing the aroma of God's grace. Someday the child will sing out with a full sound, a full overflowing heart, and begin — as it has been for all ages — the telling of his own story in the new land.

Then the nearby river will hearken and bear the tale on its voyages to the great sea. From there it is only one step to the small, quiet Hutchve which will feel the caress of a familiar hand and be surprised by joy like a mother when her child returns home.

* * *

I know that I have digressed and it is no longer customary to introduce one story before another, but our way was different. There, we didn't know which story came first and which followed. You will have to assume then that this is only a story of someone the waters carried afar and who seeks the path of yellow sand that smells of home. And meanwhile, until it is found, he tells himself stories and walks about with friends here among the mountains, on the broad meadows, the rushing rivers and smiling shores. He is beginning to feel more at home with them now, feels warmer in the bitter winter days and — you know — is even beginning to feel a longing for the nearby mountain and valley where the houses huddle in a sea of green and for the narrow stream where his child splashes year after year. Although the stories these waters tell still evade his grasp, the more he feels at home in the new land the closer does he clasp to himself the people of his home. Oh how many of their stories must he still tell himself before he feels completely at home again.

Translated from the Yiddish
by Ode Garfinkle and Mervin Butovsky

THE TRUE IMAGE

FOR SEVERAL days the priest Koznitzky had not stepped out of doors, nor even seen the light of day. When the rioting erupted and chaos ran through town like wildfire, he'd pulled shut the window-shades. He had kept them lowered after the shooting stopped. Now, oblivious to everything around him, withdrawn, turned in upon himself, he lay on the floor near his desk staring at the Christ-statue fastened to the wall.

The statue — pale white, wrought from transparent, luminous crystal — showed Jesus nailed to the cross; His pointed beard leaned lightly against His breast, and His tousled, fluttering hair conveyed a certain arrogance, recast His features in an aura of muted bitterness: *Yet I will not submit*.

Koznitzky had admired the statue from the moment he saw it. He had searched far and wide for the sculptor's name, to express his gratitude to him, his amazement that he should have captured the Redeemer's true image. *Exactly as this statue portrayed Him, Christ must have felt in His last moments:* he had sensed it in the odd crease of the brow, in the faintly perceptible sneer lurking about the stiffening lips. One thing only had disturbed him; he couldn't bear the blood-drops on the breast and on the mangled hands and feet. The longer he had thought about it, the more certain he'd been that the blood marred the integrity of the work — weakened the obdurate defiance throbbing in the taut veins.

Now, lying on the floor near his desk, his eyes fixed vacantly on the Christ-statue, Koznitzky drifted in memory, back to his boyhood, his youth....

Even as a seminary-student, he could not endure to hear Jesus described as a pushover and a sniveller. He envisioned the Lord a proud man, confronting adversity with indomitable

15

will; so he imagined Him whipping the money-changers from the temple or instructing His disciples at the Last Supper. As he grew older his vision of Jesus became clearer and more assured. At first he considered this a temptation, heresy perhaps, since wherever he looked he saw holiness convulsed in pain. The saints' despairing faces, their eyes dark under the shadow of death, overwhelmed him with futility; the renderings of Jesus treading the road to Golgotha moved him to a profound pity. But he couldn't assent to the helplessness that cried out from them. *Can that be God's Son? Was He so craven when He took upon Himself the sins of mankind?*

The idea nagged at him, relentlessly. He felt the ground slipping from under his feet and tried to save himself by confessing to the bishop. Pardon was granted him, but not peace. "My son, pictures are no more than a dim reflection of the great event. Only he who is worthy sees the true image, though he can never reproduce it."

He left the seminary soon afterwards to become a priest of his home-town church. But he couldn't escape his idea. It held him fast, pressed tighter upon him. Doubts multiplied. Night after night he sat on the veranda of his white cottage; he just couldn't understand. *Could such impotence overcome Rome, defeat Seneca and Caesar? With such humility, could they have infiltrated heathen lands and conquered them?* Unquestionably, a terrible error had been made. The secret of the man-God, the Saviour of the world, was completely misconstrued.

Afraid to make his conviction public, he secluded himself more than ever and burrowed into ancient documents, testing Latin texts against the Greek and even the Slavonic. *Somewhere here, surely,* he thought, fighting off the dread of some strange apostasy, *lies the key to the mystery, a hint of the truth.* Nothing helped. The crumbling parchments only blurred and dimmed the image he sought. And more: they made him wary of any image. At times his brain seemed to dissolve in tongues of flame. *Why torment yourself and deceive others? Get down from your ivory tower and live a little — seize the day, like other people. The Lord Himself, don't you see, got lost in His last moments and —*

He was in a bad way. Rumours buzzed through town; he overheard his parishioners whispering: "He's taking too much upon himself," "He isn't all there." They shook their heads when he passed by. "Nobody gives him any trouble here. He could shepherd the flock quietly enough. Why does he have to mix in problems above his head?" They were frightened, he knew, and were hoping for a miracle; and the miracle came in the form of a letter from the bishop. This time he found the bishop's message easier to grasp: "The image is ourselves, created in flesh and blood; we must cherish it as a living thing, and seek it in our lives. And life, my son, takes many forms."

Secure in his idea at last, he not only discarded his fear of heresy, but took courage to live by his faith. He conceived it his sacred duty to make the image manifest, to clothe it in his flesh and blood. Cautiously at first, then more explicitly and elaborately, he proclaimed his mission from the pulpit. In the astonished eyes of his listeners, and in their rapt attentiveness, he felt the world accepting his view. He grew tranquil, satisfied. One day Jan Skdjinsky, a member of the secret Organization to Free the Fatherland, took him aside and said:

"You know, father, your sermons are helping our cause. Life is flexible, father, and full of contradictions."

He didn't quite see the connection, but was glad that the younger generation had adopted his image of Jesus.

It was an especially happy occasion for him when he received the statue. A former fellow-student at the seminary sent it, one who had later broken the vow and been defrocked. In sheer joy at seeing an image of the real Jesus, he forgot to thank his benefactor or inquire about the sculptor. He hung the statue over his desk to have it always in sight. This new image of Jesus was a fine beginning; in time artists would do away with the desecrating drops of blood. Or if not, they would so transform them, infuse them with such radiance and power, as to make each drop of blood capable of shaking the very foundations of the earth. That transformation would be a victory indeed for the martyr.

Whenever he glanced at the statue his heart swelled with pride. He fancied the martyr beset by a yelping pack of pursuers — beaten and bowed down, but every twist of His bowed body expressed His contempt. To be sure, sorrow clouded His face, anguish disfigured it, yet a smile glinted from His lips (a slight, subtle smile) that laughed to scorn every one of His tormentors. The rabble raged, and He — why, He half-closed one eye in a scoffing wink, His gaze fixed on a reality transcending the turmoil around him. His lips murmured, but not the servile words recorded in scripture — not words at all, but music: melodic tones that rose tremulously, gathered, soared, and waxed in unison like a distant symphony, then distended in an infinite regression of echoing chords until they reverberated from the uttermost ends of the earth.

Many a time he thought he caught the chords. With heart beating wildly he strained to decipher their meaning: the Saviour's actual, proud words. Each time the music broke off, the image faded. There remained a gray wooden cross, and hung upon it, a grotesque figure shimmering in the swirling dark with a terrible loneliness.

Now, as he lay on the floor near his desk, withdrawn, enclosed in his fantasies and faint with hunger, Koznitzky's imagination surged with apocalyptic visions. Pagan gods straggled alongside misshapen icon-saints; alabaster-beings from Olympus contorted their bodies, twisted and writhed until they dangled from withered crosses; their wounds gaped, rancid and festering. The echo of a pistol-shot outside fused in his delirium with the thunder that resounded through that lambent evening when God's Son, solitary, wracked with pain, watched the shadows sink upon the hunched hills. From within the enveloping dusk, His pointed beard fluttered suddenly, as though to ward off some evil thing.

The priest woke with a start, and tried to take hold of himself. The spectres vanished. Nothingness thickened around him. He turned for comfort to the statue across the room, and couldn't make out where he was or what was happening. In the far recesses of his memory, fragmented phrases — his own, or another's — began to toll like church-bells: *my son ... obscured is ... the true image ... we see only ... replicas ... veiled and confused ... an illusion....* With the phrases there came phantoms. Warped figures hovered in the room, weirdly deformed, wasted, with tattered beards and gaping, foul-smelling mouths. Their wailing seemed to summon him somewhere, to something. Then a ravaged face flashed across his mind; on its lips a subtle smile mocked the passing sufferings of man.

The priest closed his eyes. Immediately the face drew near, offered itself for inspection from every angle, and he recognized it: the face of Jesus. *It must be Him. Or someone else? Chaim David, perhaps, the tailor of Tanners-Row who was tortured by the marauders just after they'd arrived in town.*

Yes, he remembered. When the riots erupted and screams from the Jews' houses rent the night, he had set forth cross in hand into the ghetto streets. Before him lamentation had filled the air, at his back the sotted raillery of marauder-soldiers and Polish legionnaires. He'd run about in cassock and surplice like one possessed, beseeching the rampant soldiers for Christ's sake not to kill. They had roared with laughter. In front of the watermill a few drunks had grabbed his cross and whipped him.

Yes, and in his terror he'd quite forgotten those notions of his about mockery, defiance, courageous forbearance. He had merely cowered — perhaps even begged; and in his soul he had repeated the plaintive words set down in scripture: "*Eli, Eli, lama sabakhtani?* My God, my God, why hast Thou forsaken me?"

Then raising himself from the dirt where he'd been flung and lashed, he had caught sight of Chaim David the tailor, a small Jew with sharp eyes and a blond beard. The tailor had stood encircled by a gang of marauders, his mouth running blood, his measuring-tape tied in a noose about his neck. He had trembled, pleaded, but with one still-open eye he gazed above the soldiers' heads and the flames that consumed the mill, gazed confidently, insolently, as though he'd seen something more essential and more real than what was going on around him.

Yes, it was as clear as day: not Jesus but Chaim David the tailor. Battered, bowed over, he had affirmed in his every twist and turn an obstinate self-assurance. Outwardly, he had begged for mercy, with bloodied lips kissed the hands of his assailants. But through it all the priest could hear him speaking in a different voice, uttering different words, an incantation — one that he, Koznitzky himself, had heard sweeping the whole night long through the ghetto streets: "*Shma Yisroel* — Hear, O Israel, the Lord is our God! The Lord is One! — *Adonoi Eloheinu, Adonoi Ekhad.*" The little Jew had not aimed the incantation against the murderers; his still-open eye had winked it, as it were, to the surrounding ghettos, across the seas, to....

A hurried knock interrupted the priest's flow of thought. He didn't get up. Let them knock, let them break the door down. He had come home determined never again to set foot outside. How could he face the world after that night? How could he lift the cross to bless his flock? He'd even smashed the one mirror he owned; how could he face himself?

Two days and two nights he had lain on the floor amid the shattered glass and stared into the void. Occasionally he'd glimpse the statue glowing in the dark. Without knowing if he was dreaming or not, he would cringe from drunken scum holding the cross over him while they whipped him and guffawed. *Jesus Mary, Jesus Mary.*

The priest closed one eye, then narrowed the other. Squinting thus his glance, like a fine dagger, cut through the drawn window-shades; in his mind's eye he scanned the ghetto streets, and suddenly running up against the blond beard of Chaim David, he seized the tailor, returned to his room, and nailed the little Jew to the statue over his desk.

Koznitzky opened both eyes wide and peered into the blackness. A new apocalyptic vision emerged. The ghetto streets sprang to life; pointed roofs grimaced at the gentile suburbs; the little houses, wobbling on decayed foundations, asserted through their slants and cracks an uncanny self-assurance. *We will prevail.* And amid the roof-tops there floated a head, slightly bowed, with a blond beard and one eye half-opened, its gaze fixed at a point somewhere beyond the entire scene, above the churning watermill, behind the blazing sun, over the lamentation that ascended from the sloping walls and mouldering wood.

"To whom, Lord? Where to?" the priest howled in a voice he didn't recognize.

The door opened. A streak of light forced its way into the room and swallowed up the shadows. Fragments of glass glittered and crackled underfoot.

"Have mercy, father, they want to kill us all!"

Koznitzky rose abruptly. He muttered garbled phrases, like a man talking in his sleep, took the statue from the wall, and lifted it to his shoulders. The three Jews followed him out, stumbling after him, stammering as they described how the legionnaires had herded all the Jews in town into the market-place and set up machine-guns for the massacre.

His torpor left him the moment he stepped outside. All his senses revived. Instinctively he tried to catch the Jews' eyes, but couldn't; he was aware as they went only of their chattering teeth and the trembling flutter of their beards.

Their panic infected him. His blood froze and boiled, boiled and froze. Yet like them he could not run, but hobbled frantically, as though lame. Like them he kept his ears open for signs that the massacre had already begun.

As they passed the church, close to the town market-place, a strange figure leaped out, clutching a broken fiddle in one hand and in the other an image of the holy Mary.

"Dear reverend sir!" He spoke in short gasps. "Are you going there too? God is with the suffering...."

The priest hurried on without answering. His heart was heavy, his mind clouded. What should he do? He could barely think. Apparitions swarmed up from his imagination, hurtled across his path and jumped aside; words like polished diamonds wrenched themselves from his lips, only to crawl back through his ears and chime with his clattering teeth; his mouth filled with rare and curious expressions for which he could find no utterance.

Directly ahead danced the bishop's golden mantilla. *Obscured is the true image; only he who is worthy sees its real form.*

Meanwhile, the ragged stranger at his side kept insisting: "If only the church-bells would start ringing, your honor, sir, they'd get scared, those devils, so help me God."

The priest hardly heard him, but the words somehow sank into his soul and entwined there with the bishop's golden mantilla. *He who is worthy sees....*

He slowed his pace, and turned dazedly from the statue to the Jews to the intruder at his side: he looked familiar. Where had he seen him before? Wasn't he a messenger of some kind? Koznitzky wanted to question him; maybe *he* had the answer. But the man was far too impassioned, too agitated, to wait.

"That's not at all how I imagined it, your worship; devils disguised as Poles." All at once, he shrilled in falsetto the well-known patriotic lyrics from Mickiewicz: "*Chemna v'shendzieh, glochoh v'shendzieh;* Darkness everywhere, silence everywhere" — and plucked the strings of his fiddle — "Who knows what will be; *Tzoh toh bendzieh.*"

Only then did Koznitzky recognize him. It was that lunatic Jan Skdjinsky, the landowner who had carried on with the secret group of freedom-fighters and praised him for coming to the aid of the fatherland. Not long ago he'd returned from somewhere or other, completely bedraggled, deranged; ever since he'd strayed about, plucking away on his broken fiddle and croaking some tune he'd made up, with verses from Mickiewicz and from the Psalms.

The priest had tried hard to avoid him. Whenever he'd seen

him wandering alone on the hills behind the church and fiddling in that madcap way, he had seemed to him the living symbol of a great tragedy. Once Jan had entered his house. He'd gazed awhile at the holy images, then strolled out into the orchard, fiddling more lonesomely than ever. When Koznitzky had asked what he wanted, he rasped: "I thought you would know when the Day of Judgement is coming."

Still, their present meeting put things in a new light. For the moment it slipped the priest's mind that this was Skdjinsky the landowner; he saw him only as the vagrant outcast who roamed the hills by day and slept in the belfry. And hearing him sing those lucid, familiar words — almost the very words he himself had so taken to heart — Koznitzky again felt the urge to question him. *He* would know something. That sombre, desultory tune, the gratings of the broken fiddle, enthralled the priest, lured him in unearthly tones.

"And what will happen if they do ring the church-bells?" he finally managed to utter.

The madman stopped short in his tracks and replied in the same declamatory falsetto, addressing the world at large: "Demons torture innocent children of the fatherland. Again our rivers run with blood; therefore the bells must ring. The day of shame has arrived!"

The priest couldn't hear him clearly because at that instant a series of high wails burst from the market-place, lifted and soared across the meadows like a flock of wounded birds. He made the sign of the cross; the three Jews began to sob in fits and starts, and mumbled incoherently, in a peculiar half-stifled paroxysm. To Koznitzky though their words took wing, joined the soaring lamentations, and together the disembodied sounds fled hastening across the woods and lake. In his mind he soared alongside them, hastening airy and light, guided in his flight by the bishop's mysterious smile. *He who is worthy sees the true image.*

They stumbled into the market-place just when the legionnaires were separating the men from the throng of women and children. Cries of pain mingled with the soldiers' raucous bellows and the neighing of horses. At one side, on the raised platform in front of the town-hall, a legionnaire beat frenziedly upon a huge drum; nearby a full company of legionnaires readied the machine-guns.

Bewildered, the priest peered about him, as though groping

in the dark. He saw at one glance the horsemen's whips crackling, the Jews' contorted faces, the hooting marauders and legionnaires. Wave upon wave of grief and mourning converged with sweat, dust, savage commands, and horses' neighing, until he was engulfed in horror. But he didn't know it — did not feel his knees giving way, the pounding in his brain, the quicksilver rushes of blood that drove him every which way. He whimpered, yowled, shook his fist, scurried from one group to another, threw himself imploringly at anyone that seemed in authority. He came to a halt, breathless, in the midst of an awful silence.

"Men! what are you doing?" With surprise he realized that it was his own voice quavering in the still air.

He heard nothing further; but he saw the legionnaires glaring at the Christ-statue, obtuse, stunned. Then a roar of outrage exploded:

"Death to the enemies of Poland!"

At that moment, like a far echo, the tolling of church-bells carried across the town, softly, then more vehemently, more shrilly, as though warning against some dire event. The priest fell to his knees, moaning, and cried with a loud voice: "So many Cains! Dear Jesus, see who really bears your cross!" He rose quickly and turned toward the frightened faces of the Jews. "It's for you, my poor brothers, that the bells are tolling. Take me among you; the Lord is with you; you are eternal." He bowed and knelt before them as before a holy image.

No one spoke; but of itself the knot of Jews uncoiled, and he was swept into its centre.

"May the Lord repay you," he murmured in an odd rasp.

The drum began to beat again, but it couldn't be heard above the tolling bells and soon fell silent.

"Death to the enemies of Christ!" someone called out. And the legionnaires, their whips flying, rifles and swords raised high, let loose in a fury at the crowd of Jews.

Arms outstretched, the priest held out the Christ-statue before the onrush. "First kill me with Him!"

The sharp glitter of a sword dazzled his eyes; as he fell to the ground his outcry reverberated through the market-place. Hastily the drum-beats began again. The tolling bells seemed strangely adrift, forlorn, like distant thunder.

Koznitzky the priest lay trampled among the murdered Jews

in the middle of the market-place, one eye half-open and bemused, the other sealed with mud. Near him, in a puddle of blood, the Christ-statue sparkled in the sun.

Translated by Sacvan Bercovitch

WHEN THE LORD WAS ANGRY

I

Prelude

IN THOSE DAYS a fiery sun blazed over the entire plain of the southern land. The springs became dry and all the wells of the surrounding countryside were like abandoned holes. The gusting east wind carried sharp burning sand-dust which turned the shrivelled plants grey and soaked up the last drop of moisture hidden in mother-earth by the nightly dew.

The earth tillers went about despondently, heads bowed to the ground, and shepherds with parched flocks wandered in the mountains searching for a spot of shady moisture in the caves and crevices of the range.

The plain was like a lime-kiln from which arose the bitter groans of women and children, the lowing of cattle and sheep.

In the mountain range amidst the holy peaks priests slaughtered sacrifices, smeared their gods with warm blood and in tumult and song bore them across the barren fields. By the glare of the moon holy virgins wandered about the mountains tearing at wild plants with bare hands, mixing them with incense and red-spices, casting them over the sacred altar-fire; heaven-seekers and star-gazers peered through the pillars of smoke to learn whether the anger of the Lord had been appeased by the atoning flames.

The priests spread their hands to the fiery heavens and chanted:

> Open your nostrils, Lord,
> And may the odour be found pleasing
> To your palate, now and forever,
> Until the smoke covers the fiery eye,
> The anger of the Lord!

In the valleys too, beneath the linden trees, blessed maidens cried their eyes out, bared their bodies to the moon, smeared themselves with oils heated in the hallowed altar-fires and pierced their flesh with sacred needles made of plaited stems.

> See, Lord, our anguish
> Dry is the womb of mother-earth
> Empty our granaries.

Thus, relentlessly, it continued night after night but still no relief arrived. Out of sorrow and fear the simple folk began to whisper:

—"The eye of the Lord is blood-red and his wrath is fierce because of the sin which plagues us day and night."

None dared speak the name of the sin though all knew its nature and source.

—"Since the days of the Flood, nothing like this has befallen our land."

—"They sported with the gods in wantonness, yet did not blaspheme."

—"They brought new customs from the desert, and woe befell us."

—"For our sins, the desert advances upon us."

But others — recalling the ancient commandment — spoke openly of the sin:

—"Was it not chiselled into the stone and bone in the holy tower in Shalem that the first-born is sacred and his blood must be united with Him through fire..."

Another challenged: "Did we inscribe a new Table of Laws?"

To which the answer came: "Remember, it was our King Malchitzedek himself who consecrated the rams and purified their horns for shofars, in honour of the Lord."

Then, spontaneously, the familiar words of the new dispensation were intoned:

> A ram for a man
> And flesh for flesh
> Shall his nostrils inhale —

Still the dissatisfied grumbled:

—"Malchitzedek read the signs from the stars and went blind..."

—"...for the sins of his children who misled us with foreign customs."

—"...with the desert dwellers did they mate, with the Hebrews, the camel-herders."

But the young people, accustomed to the new way, protested:

—"Because of their toil the land was freed, and peace reigns on earth."

Yet in their tents the elders still muttered: "The disaster comes from all directions; the desert advances toward us and consumes. Woe unto us, Malchitzedek is blind and sees not...."

Hearing this young fathers remained mute, cracked their knuckles soundlessly and shivered in their black beards. Mothers with frightened eyes heeded their first-born and with silent sadness followed the footsteps of their lords whose first-born were still unredeemed.

II

The Lady of the Hebrews sat at the entrance of her tent, quivering. Three days have passed since her Only One is nowhere to be found. Her heart is leaden; since the day her Lord withdrew himself, her precious son has always been by her side when the day wanes, and now three suns have set and he does not show himself.

Old, terribly old, is the Lady. Age has befallen her all at once. She faintly hears and dimly sees, yet from great distances she can catch the footsteps of her Only One. Even through the dense sand-dust raised by the flocks, she can see his buoyant stride coming toward her, each evening against the setting sun.

Wordlessly, he takes her hand in his and it is just as if the Lord himself would touch her. All her longing for the Master — who had left her as soon as the servant and her son were banished — surges within her when her Only One takes her hand.

Aroused by his touch she whispers to herself silently — addressing Abraham: "You know full well, my Lord, that it was not for my sake that I drove away the servant. For him, our laughing lamb, did I harden my heart to a stone and with loneliness sadden my tent. And I have no regrets." She fervently holds the silent son as if seeking to embrace her Lord's flesh with her words. "My day, Lord, is waning. In shadows do I spend my last hours, yet I am fulfilled, for each evening my son is with me — you are with me — though still so remote. He is mine entirely and you love him so because now *he* is your Only One and first-born...."

She never enquired of Isaac whether he had seen his father, nor how he was. She observed with pride how he strides toward her just as Abraham had once done. His fair hair is curled like a sheep, just like his father, but his father's hair is flaming red while her Only One's shines brightly. His father's face is harsh and lashed by the wind, the son's mild and gentle. The father's voice is clear and firm, the son's dreamy and caressing; when he speaks it is remote and filled with longing, as once her Lord's had been, when long ago while still in Ur, he had drawn her close to him by the well on the night of the new-born moon:

"Behold, my consort, you will be like the Queen of Heaven, singular, like she. Will you follow me into the distant lands too as she does?"

"Draw me close and I shall run, my Lord, my radiant one," she murmurs in the stillness — while listening to Isaac's soothing voice which seemed to emerge out of nowhere.

"On the mountaintops swirl the smoky mists. A dread hovers in the caves." Often, from within himself he would begin: "One should try to discover what lurks there, who hides himself there."

Until late at night he would recount the tales often heard from shepherds, about the caves where Grandfather Cain, his horn glowing on his forehead, had hidden himself. And about the mists into which the blessed Enoch had vanished forever, surely a sign that God himself had kissed him there amidst the peaks of the cliffs. She swallowed every word, shuddering with joy and fear: "Go not there, child, the secrets of the first days are hidden from us. See, how broad are the plains and how near the furrowed fields. The blessings of our Lord are with us here."

Once, before he caught himself, he began to speak to her, "The Lord will take me there to the mountains and into the desert, where the...."

"The Lord will take...." She quickly clasped him to herself and became silent.

Her skin shivered and with all her strength she held back the outcry. She knew that her Lord shares his days with the solitude of the desert near the Seven Wells.

There he seeks traces of the banished ones. Even now with her eyes closed she sees that blazing still morning when Hagar strode away with her overgrown howling son, wrapped in grey shawls which dragged along the sandy paths leaving narrow trails till the edge of the unknown wilderness. She saw Abraham knot and tie the sheets of the servants' tent with shaky hands and feels that even with his back turned he follows her and knots the hanging shawls into a large plait which will leave marks on all the trails. The cold she felt then penetrates her now, although the oppressive heat is everywhere.

"O my Lord," she now cries out of silent fear, just as on that morning.

For entire days and weeks the Lord has not been present in the tents. She senses his absence in the silence which envelops the entire plain. The housemaids avoid her and even Eliezer does not appear so he need not answer her questioning glance. She knows: he is drawn by those markings. He is gone to the desert. At the break of day he hurriedly saddled his ass and loaded it with leather flasks full of water, dried figs, pressed cheese and honey, and thin baked biscuits; from all provisions that are long-lasting he took small portions and stealthily stole out of the encampment before the household awakened. No one saw where he was hurrying but they all knew enough to recount from ear to ear: "His heart is filled with longing for them. He hurries to Hagar and Ishmael, to the desert of the Seven Wells. That is where he seeks them."

"The servant-woman's tread does he follow...." With great sadness she often tremulously whispered these words when loneliness painfully pressed upon her.

"His longing for the one born in his tents, leads him on," said Isaac, gently patting the hand of the wizened Lady. "His eye guards Ishmael. He wishes to make certain that the evil of the desert has not swallowed him up."

"To his tent would he come." She suddenly shuddered and in her mind's eye there formed an old familiar image. "He doesn't dismount from his donkey." A smile of pleasure creased her deep-lined face, "Ishmael the archer is not in the tent...."

"...he is on the hunt all day long," Isaac concludes the story for her as they both see the Lord bent over his donkey before an open tent. He is waiting for someone to emerge. And the longer this image lingers the clearer they both see that his entire being is transfixed in waiting in the glowing heat of the outdoors.

"And the servant-woman too does not appear," they both murmur together, and neither knows who uttered it, nor can they tell whether the words are bitter or sweet upon their tongues.

"To her own land, to Egypt, has she returned," Isaac says, remembering what he had overheard from the shepherds.

"She has purchased a wife for the archer," the lady also knows from gossip in the tents.

"The Lord's eye only wants to ascertain who is guarding the tent of his son," Isaac consoles her.

"The heart of a father." Her flesh freezes and she becomes tense in silent agony. Pain grips her and her mouth forms a reproach, but she bites her lips and remains silent. She embraces her Only One and clings to him, quivering.

It has always been thus, except now it is the third day and her Only One is not with her. Her whole being shudders. The coolness of the evening stiffens her limbs and freezes the sweat in her loose joints. Fear presses on her fluttering heart and each star-glitter in the heavens pricks her skin with fear and foreboding: "To the mountains he went, my gentle lamb. In the caves of Cain, where the Archer has concealed his den. He will ensnare him." She tears herself from the spot and runs to the middle of the field where she remains fixed, standing rigid before an unearthly apparition: the body is swathed in black shrouds, open-eyed, the void peering from them. The countenance illumined by the moon-rays is now in front, now behind, so close yet so distant, that she cannot sight it clearly. It brings tidings and each word is a knife bearing death pangs: "The Lord was in the desert." She hears the voice at close range yet from an undisclosed distance; for a long time she has known this. But now she feels impending doom on the tip of his tongue.

"And my Only One?" she wants to cry out, but remains standing rigid and silent in the surrounding darkness which suddenly envelopes her. The apparition covers itself in blackness and the pitch dark speaks to her: "The punishment which has been readied from the very beginning has come upon us because of the One and Only who has not been redeemed."

"The Lord has gone into the desert to find the first-born of his house," she responds and strides away as if to tear herself from the darkness. "He has been redeemed long ago."

"Since the desert swallowed up the Archer, my Lady, your Only One is the first-born and he has not yet been redeemed...." Again she sees the apparition before her and the voice comes from all directions: "You alone have led to this. The Lord is only doing God's will. The One and Only, whom he loves, was left unguarded by you, my Lady. So he arose in the early morning, before the mists lifted from the mountains, before the household of the Hebrews heard the sound of the shepherd's pipe. He saddled the donkey himself, took the holy brazier with the glowing coals, the flint knife, the seven-times-seven plaited rope. And loading the Only One with kindling, he left with young servants to greet the dawn in the mountains. The Master and your joyful lamb alone ascended the mountain. The donkey and the stable-boys waited behind in the valley...."

From great fear Sarah remained speechless. She stared into the darkness and saw that the unreal apparition was just an old wandering nomad, with dust on his tattered clothing and a strange story on his tongue. All her limbs were frozen and icy, only her heart shook riotously and in her temples hammers pounded.

She knows: for this was the practice of her homeland, when at dawn a father would take his eldest into the mountains. Only the mother could then guard over her son and with her own body block the father's way.

"And I did not save my Only One!" she cried shrilly as she fell to the earth and barely heard the stranger's voice. "And it was on the third morning that they approached the place. The mists came out of the caves and covered the earth so they walked heedless of a path and the silence beckoned them to the place of the holy altar. Mute is the father and grey his countenance; only the voice of the child wonders in bewilderment, "Here is the wood and here the fire, father, but where is the lamb to be sacrificed?"

"The father swallowed patches of fog and his heart shuddered with every word that reached his ear. 'The Lord sees to His lamb, my son....'

"And so they both walked until....'"

"Arise my Lady!" Faintly she hears a familiar voice waking her from a deep sleep, but she cannot tear herself from the place of the grey rock. Here is the Only One, bound, staring with wide open eyes at the overcast sky and above him the Lord with the glistening knife and outstretched arm. Red is the mist above them and the eastern horizon is aflame, where the fleeting ram's twisted horn shines in the tangled plaited branches.

"Abraham!" She rushes toward the place of the grey stone, her voice parting and driving the mists, "A lamb for a man! Here he is with his horns caught in the thicket."

"Lay not thy hand upon the child!" A voice re-echoes from all sides.

"I will never again stand in your way, Lord," she sobs, her quivering hands reach out to him. She feels as if her whole being is extended to that place, lying with her Only One on the readied pile of kindling, his eyes blinded by the red sky.

"My Lady!" The same voice continues to wake her. With difficulty she opens her eyes to see Eliezer standing in the tent's opening, tidings on his lips.

"... the Master has returned from the mountains."

"And the..." She does not manage to complete the sentence, and her ear does not catch Eliezer's joyful words.

"The Only One is with him and also the youths who went with them. The earth is blessed and the eldest son of the Hebrews is redeemed with the Lord's blessing for the whole land. From this time forward every eldest on the whole plain is redeemed. See, the rain is hurrying from the west and the earth will be quenched with the blessing of the sky. Arise, my Lady, I hear the Lord and the redeemed One approaching!" Eliezer suddenly sensed that his mistress no longer heard him. With a terrified cry, he tore at the flap of the tent:

"My mistress! ... Hurry, Lord of the Hebrews!"

"My Only One!" With a shudder, she whispered her last, stretching out her trembling hands in a half circle as if to embrace someone.

Under the open sky a donkey brayed unearthily as Eliezer stumbled backwards from the tent wailing with death-fear: "The Lady!"

Translated from the Yiddish by
Ode Garfinkle and Mervin Butovsky

LIGHT IN THE DARKNESS

A memorial for the hearth-keeper Mikolai, who remained a man in a time of beasts.

THROUGH a gap in the cemetery fence old Mikolai watched the shtetl being emptied. Tangled knots of people, the town's Jews, scurried by the fence, shouldering their dishevelled packs and bundles, leaving behind dust clouds and the mounted cossacks who pursued them, sabres drawn. The sun was pitiless and the landscape looked parched and wilted.

Mikolai lay huddled on the ground, dazed, his misty eyes studying the scene. Like the dust clouds rising and settling, his thoughts were scattered, in disarray. More than once he had struggled to call to mind the appearance of the shtetl, without success. He only knows that it is Friday and he must set out to sweep the Jewish shul, but he cannot remember what the shul looks like. Just then, another shapeless cluster of people, dust, wailing, swirled past the cemetery, followed by a frightening silence. The abrupt stillness momentarily cleared his mind. *Yes, it is Friday: he is on his way to sweep out the shul with a fresh broom. Playful children chase after him, teasing:*

> *Mikolai, Mikolai,*
> *Want a bun?*
> *See us run!*

Smiling goodnaturedly, he raises his broom toward them; they vanish instantly into the dust-clouds. Confounded, he rubs his bloodshot eyes but sees only his familiar hut shrouded in awful stillness. With a mighty effort he begins to recall the recent events. For three whole days he had remained in his hut. As soon as the first detachment of cossacks occupied the shtetl he shut himself within his four walls and never ventured out. Little Zushka, who looked after him, brought him the news. Soon he had no need to be told, for the startling outcries which came to him in the middle of the night revealed more than her reports. Each time the shrieking from the far side of the bridge reached him, he would crawl off his straw pallet and lie down alongside the fence, listening attentively. Lying there, he would completely forget where he was. It seemed that he was still a young boy stretched out on the straw in his father's barn at the edge of the Lipowitzer forest, listening to the shrill, inhuman cries borne out of the black woods. He could recognize, by the sound of each shriek, which helpless creature was being devoured. Now too, his hearing was poised to catch the outcries rising in the night from the Jewish alleyways.

Mikolai, a kind, affectionate grandfather, liked to hold Zushka on his lap and tell her about the years gone by, the heroic national struggle, the tales of young people long ago. He could not understand why foreigners had suddenly taken to interfering in the life of the shtetl, disturbing everything. Being an earnest, hardworking man, he could not fathom how, in the middle of everything, in the midst of summer when the work was burning, people could allow themselves to go about empty-handed and foment trouble. "Idle hands are the cause of these things," he told himself, struggling to understand. "Naturally, when people hang about chewing the air with nothing to occupy them, they can only cause trouble."

His mind grew befuddled at such concentrated thought and he fell lightly asleep where he lay by the fence. He awakes with the first rays of the sun and shuffles into his hut, remaining on the straw pallet for the rest of the day without the least desire to go outdoors. By the third day, when the tumult was loudest and the women's howling broke into his hut, he could bear it no longer and crawled out to the fence.

Dread overwhelmed him. The entire shtetl, young and old, bunched into one wailing throng, straggled along the road by the cemetery. Some broke away from the pack and stretched their hands through the palings of the fence. The cossacks swiped at the outstretched hands with bared blades. That sight tore something within him. Everything became confused and he could no longer distinguish what was happening now from what had happened long, long ago.

They are driving out the Jews. It was as if his mind had received a hammer blow. *They are taking their farewell from their dead.* His whole being was stirred by their sobbing. *I alone will care for their ancestors.* He read their final plea in the desperate hands clutching the fence.

Dazed and stupefied, he began crawling on all fours, searching in the high grass that bordered the fence. *I must hide the hacked-off fingers with their own kind.* This thought burned his mind like fire. He found nothing. Weary and bewildered, he lowered himself to the ground behind the fence.

From the depth of his memory a story surfaced, a bible story that told of a people driven into exile by their enemies' scourges. Faint and starving, they arrived at the border of a distant kingdom, where the inhabitants greeted them with bread and herring, stilling their hunger pangs. The suffering exiles rejoiced, thankful for the provisions. They took consolation, too, in the friendly reception of the strangers. "See," they said to one another, "good people are to be found in distant lands." But soon they were overcome by thirst and instead of water were given inflated sheep-bladders to suck, which they drew upon, swallowing the dank air until their stomachs burst in great agony. The old man clutched himself and buried his face in the grass; yes, he remembers every detail. The bible story had been told to a class of boys by the Reader in the white church, ages and ages ago. "And the corpses of the persecuted lay on the sands of the desert until jackals made a feast of their rotting flesh." The fearful picture painted by the Reader is still clear in his mind. He even remembers that he became nauseous and fainted away, and the Reader — a faithful Christian, may he enjoy a blessed paradise — revived and comforted him. "Mikolai, you will grow up to be a good Christian, you have a pure heart. But the bible story is only a parable about the body and the soul...."

From moment to moment he recalls more. He can't understand why it is called a "parable," for it has just happened, their cries are still in the air. They are already at the desert sands. He scrambled to his feet and ran into the hut. It was filled with an oppressive quiet like the mute silence of a creature with a thousand sorrows in its eyes. The stillness caught him pincerlike, holding him fast. Then it seemed that the entire hut began to babble in a mysterious tongue, hooting and ululating as if alive. Seized by an overpowering fear, he fled outside again to hide.

Near the door he tripped over the pitcher, now empty, which was always filled with water in readiness for the visitations of the dead, who came nightly to cleanse their hands. Shoilke the gravedigger replenished the container each morning with fresh water. *It has been three days since the pitcher was filled.* He shuddered at the thought. In the past he would never dare touch it. "The Jewish dead," his father had warned, "want to be attended by their own kind." But they cannot be left behind, abandoned, without water. All his affection for the shtetl and its Jewish townsfolk swelled within him and a strong, stubborn resolve formed: he would take on the duty, he would care for the deserted dead just as if the living were still here.

The fervour of his decision renewed his strength and he filled two pitchers and placed them on either side of the path leading to the graves. The action rid him of his earlier fears, his spirits rose and once again he felt bound to the shtetl. The peaceful days of the past emerged, the hushed Sabbath daybreak when he hastened to heat the shul. He sees before him the festive, humming gathering of worshippers deeply immersed in chanting their devotions. This scene always brought him pleasure, but at the same time troubled him. *They know all their prayers by heart and have no need of a Reader, not like the peasants, who are blind and won't make a move without the priest, even in reciting their prayers.* Those Sabbath mornings aroused in him a respect for Jews, and suffused with contentment he would fervently cross himself behind the oven and hurry from house to house to warm up the shtetl. By noon he would be on his way home, head spinning and warm from whisky, carrying a sack filled with chunks of cake and egg loaf. No wonder the Sabbath was a holy and pleasurable day for him, its special grace lasted all week long. He never liked the summer Sabbaths and out of spite would do nothing all day but lie about on a straw pallet, yawning. "It's really not a Sabbath at all, just a long, drawn-out day." It made him feel useless. But winter days reinvigorated him and he felt he was the centre of the entire shtetl: it is more than mere neighbourliness, they simply can't manage without him. Sometimes gangs of Polish boys would taunt him on the church steps. "Mikolai, have you had it snipped off already?" He wouldn't deign to answer, rebuking them instead with a glance which said: *What can you know, you blockheads.*

Suddenly he came to a halt, his heart warm, his face radiant. He saw the children dancing around him on a Friday afternoon. "Mikolai, Mikolai, recite the Thanksgiving Prayer!" Leaning on the tall broom he chuckles goodheartedly: "Tatenu,

Mamenu, Moidi Ani, Amen." The youngsters enjoy his familiarity with their prayer and encircle him, dancing the hopke while he melts with pleasure. "Sweet children, how well you've looked after yourselves. Swimming in summer, snug by the oven in winter. Come tomorrow and I'll give you some Sabbath treats," he calls out in Yiddish. Startled by his own words, he realizes that he is standing before his hut, alone.

A moment later he is at the shed where the brooms are stored. He selects the fullest and tallest and begins to steal through the back alleys leading toward the shul. In the Friday dusk the lifeless, abandoned shtetl catches his footsteps and re-echoes them through the emptiness. Fear grips him and before he knows it he finds himself creeping on the ground close by the plundered houses. With the broom on his back he crawls on all fours, too frightened to raise his head, to look at his houses, so bare and desolate. His heart is torn: this town had been a living being full of houses and people — his people — and without warning everything is gone. The houses are grave-stones. He wants to enter them but is afraid to veer from the path and keeps moving forward. His eyes moisten over. Even when Maria died — may she have a blissful paradise — he had been unable to shed tears. He could only clasp Zushka to his heart and whisper, "Now we are both orphans, Zushka." The little one had sobbed; he couldn't bring up more than warm spit. Now he spilt tears. Crawling and weeping, he collided with the corner of a house and realized where he was. He considered turning back, but his firm resolve stood in the way: he would guard the shtetl. Beyond the graveyard fence lay the old dead shtetl and here he would stay with what was left behind.

On the threshold of the shul he came upon crazy Fayge Layah sitting stiff and unmoving. At other times he would have driven her away, but now he was overjoyed: a remnant of the shtetl. In the prayer-house everything was as before except that the sacred books were gone, and the bare bookcases stared at him like insulted, humiliated children. He turns his head away from them and begins to sweep, doing his work earnestly, but his heart is hollow, something gnaws so strongly. The sight of the dusty, unpolished chandeliers is unbearable and he hurries to shine them, wiping around the water-barrel too. Soon, everything is in readiness to receive the Sabbath. He sits near the oven, waiting.

From the vestibule crazy Fayge Layah sings her mournful lament, whose words he knows by heart:

> All who were beautiful, all who were gracious
> Have already departed,
> O, O, O, Momma,
> Let us go to meet the Messiah
> Let us not tarry...

Among all the Yiddish words, only the meaning of the Hebrew "Messiah" escapes him, but he knows the melody and hums along out loud. Hearing his voice, Fayge Layah bursts angrily into the prayer-house to find Mikolai beaming amidst the polished interior. Something flickers in her fevered brain and for a moment she seems to grasp what is taking place. She throws him a demonic look, a look recently plucked from a sealed world, a look with the power to unveil any human disguise. Mikolai shuddered. He felt his knees begin to buckle, his hands automatically raised themselves to cross his heart while he silently murmured: "In the name of the Father, the Son, and the Holy Ghost...."

Fayge Layah was no longer attentive. She threw herself at the Holy Ark. Finding it empty of Torah scrolls, she howled in anguish and plunged down the steps, thrusting her unkempt head between her knees as she wailed and moaned indecipherable phrases.

Her howls roused Mikolai. He saw the shul engulfed in darkness. With a feeling of serenity he shuffled to the cantor's lectern and lit the remaining bits of candle in the candelabra, then clambered onto a bench and, imitating the pious gestures of the sexton, lit the stubs of candles in the chandelier. The flaming candles drove segments of darkness into the corners, filling him with rueful sorrow and dread.

Without warning, a cossack patrol burst through the door, murderously fell upon Mikolai, who stood enchanted, his smile radiant.

"Trying to signal the enemy, you cursed Jew!"

Before Mikolai could answer, a blow from a rifle butt silenced him forever.

The madwoman lunged toward him but was held by the surprised patrol, who shouted lustfully, "A woman, grab her!"

Powerful arms held her, stuffed her mouth and carried her

to the vestibule. Stifled grunts sounded from her. The crazed heat coming off her wrinkled skin further aroused her captors. The frantic struggle became more urgent and tense. Then for an instant the gag was squeezed out of her mouth and she roared with all the strength of madness: "Momma!"

The cry sliced the darkness like lightning. The uniformed soldiers felt that a hissing flame had scorched their bodies, rendering them helpless and confused. A moment later they were slouching through the darkened lanes, heads lowered, observed only by the blank window panes of the houses. Flames guttered in the shul alone. Released from her ravishers, Fayge Layah lunged back into the shul, brought a dipper of water to the dying Mikolai and wet him with her tears.

The madness seemed to withdraw from her. The mind suddenly grasped everything, and the eyes — glowing like an angry wildcat's — pierced the gaping, empty Holy Ark, as she cried out, blaspheming: "Shabbos! Shabbos!"

Translated by Ode Garfinkle and Mervin Butovsky

THERE WAS A MAN

WHEN the Days of Awe arrived Esther and Srulche, together with all the other settlers from the villages, journeyed to the nearby shtetl. Esther took her place just inside the door of the women's shul and Srulche stood by the door of the men's shul. This is where all the other transients, villagers, and unschooled simple folk gathered to pray. Usually, no one paid attention to them except for the sexton who would frequently approach one of them glancing into the prayer-book to see if the reader had the correct place. The villager would become embarrassed and cover his head with his prayer shawl. Srulche stood without a prayer-book, his eyes closed, quietly swaying and murmuring. When mischievous youngsters saw him, they surrounded him giggling, waiting for the right moment to shout at him, "You yokel!" But when he opened his eyes they sensed such an unworldly brightness that he was left in peace.

At one time Srulche moved to the anteroom to pray along with the tradesmen. When Esther asked why he had forsaken the shul, he said, "The beady eyes of the parnass pierce us through and through, and the property-owners preen themselves with their learning. But the eyes of the tradesmen warm us with their hospitality. Even with their prayer-books held upside down, their devotions have deeper feeling."

As soon as the village population increased, they decided to form their own minyan. The villagers were overjoyed. Now they would no longer have to leave all their belongings in the care of their gentile neighbours, nor would they have to suffer the disdainful glances of the townspeople in the streets, or be exposed to their side-long stares when they fumbled clumsily with city spoons. And more importantly, they would no longer have to be in mourning in order to be called to read from the Torah, nor quake in fear at the prospect of making an error in the recitation. Only one problem remained: where would they find someone they could call their Moreinu — their learned guide and teacher. They had presumed that they were never called to Torah readings because only the Moreinus — those with solemn Days of Awe faces, prayer-shawls raised above their necks — were summoned to the pulpit; that only a Moreinu was called to the Torah. And where would they find such a teacher! Amongst themselves they had decided that Srulche, who could carry a tune, would lead the services from the pulpit and become their teacher.

In fact, this is what happened and the villagers enjoyed festive Days of Awe. Srulche chanted the prayers with such sweet understanding that every fibre of their bodies melted in rapture. Everyone was called to the Torah, and no longer fearing alien eyes which anticipated their mistakes, they stumbled through the blessings in peace. That made it a real holiday. They hardly felt that these were solemn days because the world about them appeared so beautiful. At summer's end thousands of red and yellow colours sported, and on the harvested fields — which looked like chin-stubble on unshaven peasants — there stretched spider-web filaments which sparkled in the sun like white silk. These signalled the moment for wintry winds to begin to blow. In the meantime joy reigned in the fields. Potatoes were dug up and cabbages harvested. There was a rich odour of heavy toil and the promise of certain sustenance. The villagers caught the scent and responded to the prayers as if they were tasty dishes which melt in the mouth. They sang out lustily, chopping the stubborn Hebrew words like a baler-blade cutting straw. The peasants stopped before the tavern where the services were held. They were pleased: "The Zhids are confessing. Our labour is lightened knowing that when we work others are praying to their God." And those peasants familiar with the villagers shouted into the tavern, "Pray neighbours, pray to your own and assure us a mild winter. Pray!"

The villagers responded with a noisier garbling of the Hebrew prayers while Srulche elaborated a new trill to the melody of the liturgy. For the first time in their lives the villagers experienced such fervent praying.

And what was the result of all this? Everything took a turn for the worse. For when the townsfolk realized what the villagers had done, the parnass ordered them to come immediately to the city to answer the charge of organizing a minyan without authorization from the community council. The celebration of Succos was spoiled. On Succos eve Srulche and the other villagers appeared in the prayer-house in their stocking-feet to ask forgiveness of the parnass and the trustees. All the townspeople gathered near the windows and ridiculed the villagers as they stood in the Beis Medrash with darkened faces, their tongues stammering, unable to open their mouths properly.

The trustees and parnass deliberated for a long while, arguing among themselves until they finally asked who had led the services. Srulche hesitatingly stepped forward and they began to question him on matters of liturgy. Not all of his answers found favour with the opinions of his examiners, provoking grimaces and furrowed brows. Noting these, the surrounding crowd abandoned all restraint and their derision, cast over the heads of the villagers, gathered like a heavy load. Some of the villagers bent beneath the weight, while others, unable to contain themselves any longer, wanted to strike blows. Srulche barely held them back as he turned to address the trustees.

"Where we come from," he said, "it is brighter than it is here."

"What nerve!" said the parnass angrily, "the likes of this has never been heard before."

At this, even Srulche could not control himself. "Don't you see, trustees? There is such a great world of wonders and only petty hands obscure it..."

The parnass exploded with anger and he threatened Srulche with fines and whippings. But the trustees were more sympathetic for they sensed a quality in his voice beyond the spoken words, and searching for a compromise, they charged the villagers with supplying wood for the Beis Medrash for the winter. From that time Srulche acquired a title: the villagers now called him Reb Srulche the Innkeeper.

At the same time Alexei — with whom Srulche had earlier shared a hut in the forest — returned from his wanderings. He was affectionate and cordial, speaking calmly and softly to everyone. The peasants respected him because he told them of the holy places, and had a ready proverb for every occasion. Frequently, he and Srulche wandered off for several days. When he returned he would be full of wonderful tales of the herbs they had discovered which could heal the sick. Villagers and peasants from the surrounding countryside began to approach the innkeeper, asking advice and seeking remedies. Srulche would hide from them, but so many supplicants were cured that others refused to leave him alone. His reputation was carried to distant regions where they had heard about the holy man — the Baal Shem — who lives in a village and heals with roots and herbs. They called him the Baal Shem — Master of the Name — for it was their custom to use that title for those, who in God's name, performed healing deeds with herbs. Srulche, however, continued to hide himself from the people. So they searched for him in the adjoining woods, amidst the cliffs; but they rarely found him when he sought to remain hidden. He was aided by Alexei, who, being familiar with the Baal Shem's hiding places, cunningly steered the seekers to other locations.

But the needy were not as easily misled and they would sit for days and weeks waiting the opportunity to meet him. When they returned home they had marvellous tales to tell of what they had heard and seen of the innkeeper who hides in the mountains. The scholars and well-to-do shrugged their shoulders, and even mocked; others maintained that he should be summoned before a tribunal in order to reveal his identity. The simple folk, however, were drawn to him and sought him out. They laid their complaints and troubles before him and drew consolation from his words.

Many beseeched him to settle in the town, but he would always avoid a clear answer. But once, on a frosty day, through the window of his house he saw a company of Jews approaching. He knew their purpose immediately and fled through the back door into the hills.

A white world glistened in the sun. Trees covered in translucent icicles peered down into the valley. The entire landscape was a silent world expectantly waiting. From time to time an animal raised its head from a burrow, then fearfully hid again. Srulche felt uneasy. Something was lacking, something which he could not describe. His restlessness increased from moment to moment and he felt trapped. All about him were mountain peaks crowned with snow, a dazzling white world enveloped in a blue crystalline firmament. Almost imperceptibly he fell into the snow and lay there confused, muttering to himself, "Where shall I go now? What shall I do?" And lying there he was overcome by a profound longing, a craving to embrace everything, to inhale it all and be at one with it. The longing drew him and tore him from the spot, dispersing his confusion and despair. He saw before his eyes the attic where he had spent his childhood. He felt the caress of Buba Tzivia's bony hand and heard her voice from a far, far, distance. "Did you think Srulche, that Jewish hopes had been in vain?" And now Zhamele, with his smiling face, appears before him. "What are you doing lying here, Srulche, the world is so open and broad. Arise!" And suddenly he is in the shul's anteroom, behind the oven. A red flame shines from the oven door and behind his back someone stands looking at him with love.

Soon everything vanishes and he is now in Brod. In the small Beis Medrash where he formerly prayed, it is crowded, airless. Everyone sits close together, listening to the simple words of a stranger, who is tall and odd-looking. "Who is this man? Isn't he the one who will not allow himself to be addressed as 'Rebbe,' but simply 'Leib Sarah's.' Srulche wished to observe the man closely, to examine the tall Jew, but he abruptly disappeared from view, and when he raised his eyes he saw that night had fallen. A star-studded world rose above him, wrapped in the hushed mystery of mountain and valley. And within him too, there fell a calm stillness, a feeling of grace and serenity which welled up and streamed within.

"It is so beautiful on this earth —" he murmured to himself, and started back to the village.

Suddenly a cry from the distance, from the forest. It was the howl of ravenous wolves hunting their food, their prey. The forest was aroused. Defenceless animals, in a dead fright, darted about noisily, seeking a hiding-place. A sadness enveloped Srulche. His former lucid vision evaporated and all that remained was a sympathetic feeling for mankind: to approach them through tales, to speak with them. He did not see clearly what he was to say, but something drew him and he felt he would speak. His pace quickened and as he passed his barn and heard the quiet lowing of the cows it seemed to speak softly to him, saying, "You must depart. You must return to home and kindred."

So he departed and at home found a group of Jews anxiously awaiting. When he appeared they could not look at him directly, so radiant had he become. He could not understand

47

why they did not meet his eyes and he rebuked them. "People should look directly at one another." They grew ashamed and remained silent. But one of them detached himself from the gathering and complained, "Why do you hide yourself from us?"

The query so penetrated his being, stabbing him through and through, that he immediately felt himself free from the burden of concealment. All at once, it seemed that the disguise which had hidden him for so long, fell away. It became easier to look at the group, but he felt their sharp and cutting gaze like a keen slaughter-knife. Such beseeching, down-cast glances. He knew they had come to plead, to implore for something, yet he could see that they still did not dare, that a wall still separated them. This brought him even closer to them, but he could utter no more than a question.

"Why have you come?"

"We heard your name, which is famous in our region," said the same questioner, haltingly meeting his eyes.

"Go into the fields and you will see beauty. Go into the forest and you will hear how He lives among his creatures. There is such joy, there is —"

"While we on Bath Street are dying from hunger and fear," the other cut him off.

"Who are you and what do you want?"

"Everyone calls me Leib Sarah's, and I tell you it is not enough to sit in the mountains and see how the forests live. Come and see how the Jews live."

At these words the crowd swayed in fear because Srulche's face became pale, then turned livid. At that moment Alexei thrust his way through the people and stood beside him.

"They are right, Srulche. Even in the village they are suffering from hunger and fear."

"Then a little happiness must be brought to them," Srulche called out.

"Yes," shouted Reb Leib Sarah's in joy, "Yes, Baal Shem."

"We must bring them joy," said Srulche, repeating the words to himself.

A stone was lifted from the hearts of the crowd, and one of them, so carried away that he could not tell whether he dreamt or was awake, started to sing an ecstatic niggun. He threw out one phrase, then the crowd picked up the melody prolonging the humming from one theme to another. The melody veered from joy to solemnity, from solemnity to exhilaration, like passing from the dark nightmare which devours a person beyond all reason, to the sudden burst-through of the sun; or when happiness is suddenly regained through the appeal of a child's sweet face, and the soul brightens, full of hope and joy. That is the way the niggun unfurled. No one could tell where it began or ended. It arose out of itself, from out of the soul, a chant fulsome and rapturous, telling of the discoveries which only its own language could enunciate, which only the niggun without words, could voice.

And when the morning star shone palely through the window they began to move as though by instinct toward the door, setting out on the roadway to the shtetl. Esther stood by the door crying with gladness. As Srulche passed her he looked lovingly into her eyes. She sobbed louder, so he bent over and quietly whispered, "Esther, it must begin in joy."

No one really understood why they made such haste to be off to town so early, but they all felt that they should leave without delay. Everyone wanted to arrive at the earliest with the tidings: They had found him. And Reb Leib Sarah's was certain that he had discovered the one who, with joy, would thaw the freezing poor in all the vestibules. He hurried the people along.

"Sing out Jews! The hidden-one has been revealed. All will be light, Jews. Sing out, as only you know how!"

Sleepy wood-cutters, rushing through the woods, stopped and gazed in amazement. Seeing their "Holy Neighbour" — the term they used for the innkeeper — amidst a crowd of Jews, they grasped fully what was happening and threw themselves on him, pleading.

"You are forsaking us Holy One? Who will remain with us?"

He had no time to answer because Reb Leib Sarah's caught sight of Alexei standing at the entrance to the forest weaving a chair of twigs. He ran toward him in high spirits.

"On this chair of simple twigs, among the simple folk, take your place, Rebbe!"

Later, no one could tell who had first seated the Baal Shem on the chair of twigs. But when they recovered from the bliss that had filled their souls, when they sensed the final notes of their niggun — which no one could ever recall again — the sun was already shining, drenching the earth in cisterns of light which reflected off the icicled trees, spreading a festive splendour over the whole world.

And the chair of twigs, raised on high over the heads of the surging crowd, moved on toward the shtetl.

Translated from the Yiddish by
Ode Garfinkle and Mervin Butovsky

THE FAR SIDE OF THE RIVER

AFTER THREE days, the Soviet horsemen stormed the town. Through key-holes and cracks in the attics, the inhabitants watched the entry of the band of riders on small horses. They looked more like a cheerful, carefree gang than a regular army, arrayed in their bizarre outfits: red Russian blouses and short pants, ankle-length noblemen's overcoats and silk dressing gowns. Some were in ladies jackets and blouses, topped with chapeaux and fur hats. Others wore high silk top-hats, or bound their heads in brilliant kerchiefs. Most were barefoot, or in split boots, their toes showing.

They galloped into town singing. If it had not been for their outstretched guns, they could have been taken for a band of costumed merry-makers coming to town for a good time.

"The barefoot gang," was the nickname someone attached to them, and it stuck, even after the regular army units had appeared in proper military formation and regulation uniforms.

"The bigger the hole, the higher the rank," was how the villagers joked about the officers, whose clothing was no different than all the others.

"If you want to tell who an officer is, count the holes in his trousers."

The nickname was not intended to belittle the new rulers, but seemed an expression of grateful relief. After all, here were familiar fellows with whom one had recently traded at the fair, clasped hands with over a deal, and downed a glass together. Even the officers didn't put on airs.

The riders came to a halt in the middle of the market place. As agile as a cat, one of them sprang from his horse to the fire-bell post near the well, and climbing quickly to the top, tied a small red flag. Then, just as deftly, he jumped back into his saddle.

Almost immediately, the populace cautiously emerged from their hiding places. The terrors of the previous night, when the retreating Polish army had blown up the bridges and military barracks, passed. The joyous singing of the newly-arrived Soviets dispersed the lingering echoes of the terrified cries which had revereberated through the town in recent days, cries which had arisen from the dark, locked houses where the retreating Polish soldiers had rampaged.

At first warily, then hurrying as if anxious not to be late, people began streaming into the market square from all quarters of the town. From somewhere in a back alley, a group of civilians suddenly appeared carrying a large red flag and singing "The Internationale." The riders joined in the singing, and many by-standers who had earlier been uncertain, stepped briskly toward the market like guests rushing to a wedding.

In the square, everything was unusually clean and orderly. The darkened closed shops did not arouse fear; instead, they lent a festive Sabbath air to the market. The square rapidly filled with a happy, good-humoured crowd. People mingled with the soldiers, talking and laughing heartily, like old acquaintances.

Suddenly, a slender young man whose thick moustache added a stern touch to his gentle face, appeared on the balcony of the old brick house in the market place. Without a jacket, one leg of his underwear tattered about the ankle, he looked like a jester. His authoritative bearing, however, made an impression. Everyone fell silent when he snatched his quilted cap — its padding showing through split seams — and flung it brusquely aside.

"As commandant of your town," he began in fluent Polish, "I salute the Red Army on her great victory over the aristocrats and bourgeoisie. We haven't come to take the land away from the peasant and worker; we've come to free you because we know of your oppression. We will help you build a free and happy Poland."

"Long live freedom!" thundered voices in several languages.

"Long live a liberated Poland!" Throats strained until they became hoarse.

Amidst the tumult, some of the more circumspect of the townsfolk detached themselves from the crowd and scurried homeward. Whatever happened, no need to get too closely involved. Over the alleyways hung a fearful silence, a tension heavy with misgiving; its presence was soundless, but it lurked everywhere, all eyes. And it was those eyes that caused people to shudder and hide themselves as quickly as they could, in their own corner.

"Who knows what will come of this?"

"Certainly another type of Russian, but who can trust them?" others grumbled.

Toward evening however, after the commandant's final words had been relayed from house to house — that tomorrow morning all stores would be reopened, and that all goods purchased would be paid for in full — the townsfolk's hearts felt lighter.

"... and those caught looting will be shot on the spot." These words both pleased and yet frightened them, with their reminder that danger had not passed. Yet, on the whole, they were more assured. They even dared to go out at night in front of their houses, and later, to venture as far as the market place. And when the night patrol confined people to their homes, they accepted the curfew as reasonable, gratified that order was being restored. Hope in free and better days grew along with the quiet of the night. After the long weeks of fear and trembling, a great many townsfolk went to sleep relaxed and secure in their own beds, and actually undressed fully, just like normal times.

Next morning at early dawn, Chaim and Shternberg ran all over town trying to locate the commandant in order to obtain permission to make their way home. The streets were as crowded and noisy as a bustling country fair. Soldiers with great bundles of goods under their arms were pushing their way from shop to shop, paying for their purchases with paper money which they cut from sheets with scissors. Groups of soldiers gathered in front of stores that remained closed and shouted until from somewhere or other the proprietor was brought forward. Within an hour or two the store was completely emptied. The shopkeeper stood in front of his bare shelves, a bewildered witness, wondering what was to be done with the pieces of green and red paper — their designated value running to the hundreds of thousands — printed on only one side. Some soldiers simply pulled out large sheets of ruled graph paper, tore off one or two squares, and handed them to the shopkeepers as payment. The situation was chaotic.

Shopkeepers ran about, pleading their case to passing officers. Anyone who looked official was pulled into the shops to see for themselves. But nothing seemed to help.

"We're being slaughtered without knives," the shopkeepers groaned, and beseeched anyone they knew, "take away as much as you can carry. At least let me try to save a little something. What will I do with all this toilet paper?"

By midday, most of the shops were stripped bare, and the shopkeepers stood at their doorways nervously pulling and chewing their disshevelled beards. They were not permitted to close their shops; this was seen to by the guards who were posted on duty, ostensibly to prevent robberies.

Soon, freshly printed posters in several languages made their appearance, announcing that a Revolutionary Committee had been established to govern the town, and advising all inhabitants to loyally obey the new regime. Furthermore, it announced that within twenty-four hours all possessions must be declared, including any firearms — loaded or unloaded — which must be surrendered to the Committee without delay. Those who disobeyed would be punished according to revolutionary law.

All at once, the civilian population vanished from the market square. Only the bewildered shopowners, fearful and gloom-laden, trembled in their shops. From time to time they ran to the windows and peered into the square, then, for no obvious reason, returned to their positions behind the counter, near the empty shelves. Out of the side alleys, militiamen wearing red arm-bands led frightened prosperous Jews and Poles. They hurried across the market place and disappeared into the magistrate's stone house, where the commandant, his staff, and the Revolutionary Committee were quartered. Wild rumours filled the air.

"They are taking hostages."

"They are rounding up forced labourers."

"They have demanded a tax."

"They are arresting the young people."

"They will confiscate all our belongings."

"They will soon withdraw."

"Soon there will be shooting."

"The Polish legionnaires have already been spotted on the other side of the bridge."

From minute to minute the fear mounted. Despairing

shopkeepers, who had been waiting for the opportune moment when the patrolmen looked the other way, stole out of their shops and disappeared into the back lanes where doors and shutters opened hurriedly, then slammed shut once again. With wife and child, they crawled down to the cellars, or up to the attics, or exhaustedly, lay down on the floor in a dead fright.

The panic also encompassed the guards, who, poised for attack with bayonets outstretched, advanced along the walls searching for concealed enemies.

In the midst of this terror, Chaim and Shternberg managed to separate themselves from the throng in the brick house. They pushed from room to room, vainly looking for the commandant. No one would tell them who the commandant was, nor where he might be found. Then, just as they were about to step over the threshold to leave, the guards suddenly stopped them, and they were brought before him.

In a corner of a wide corridor, a young man half-dressed in military garb and chewing zestfully on an apple, smilingly faced them.

"Now everything is free," he said, after hearing the appeal. "You can travel wherever you wish." He spoke through a mouthful of apple, as he walked to the door with long strides.

Chaim, however, did not let him go, and with humble peasant innocence, begged, "I'm a poor peasant, tovarish. The Poles captured us and dragged us — myself and the children's tutor — to this town. It took nine of them to hold us, believe it or not, and I'm afraid they will arrest us again. It's about thirty kilometres from here to the other side of the Bug. Please give me a piece of paper so your comrades will let us pass." Chaim followed the commandant, speaking at his shoulder blades.

"A Jewish peasant?" The commandant stopped abruptly and offered his outstretched hand to Chaim. "Shalom Aleichem, Reb kinsman, and where are your horses?" He spoke with a distinctive Vohlynian Yiddish accent. "Why didn't you tell me immediately that you are not from these parts?"

"The horses were taken from us," Chaim said, shrugging his shoulders. He too switched to Yiddish, his entire bruised face with its plucked-out beard, grinning with pleasure. "Please give us a paper."

"Just look at this pest," the commandant grumbled. "You've already been told that you don't need a permit to travel."

"But we're afraid," Chaim persisted.

"Oh, so you're afraid? Then go recite Kri-Shma if that's any help," the commandant said, grinning and measuring them from head to toe with his gaze. "Those Poles really gave you a good going over — may the devil devour their entrails. Here, give me your back, comrade, and you'll get the paper that will take you all the way home."

"Back home they think we have already departed this world," Chaim said, much at ease.

"No doubt," said the commandant as he pulled a piece of yellow wrapping paper from his pocket, and using Shternberg's back for a desk, began scribbling a few words.

"Here, take this; it will be good enough without a seal. Just say that Avrunin gave his permission. They won't stop people like yourselves, but just in case they do, just show this paper." And turning quickly, he was no longer there.

When they came outside, slightly confused and befuddled with excitement, the panic seemed to be over. Militiamen and soldiers were going from house to house, calming the people.

"Everything is under control, citizen-comrades. Only enemies spread wild rumours. This evening come to the synagogue or church and you will be told about everything. The common people need have no fear; only the bourgeoisie and the noblemen should be quaking in their boots!"

At dusk, when Shternberg approached the Great Synagogue, the doors were wide open, but it was impossible to get in. It was densely packed. Several penny-candles sputtered in the two remaining chandeliers which swayed on long wires that extended from the domed ceiling. The Eternal Flame facing the cantor's dais flickered in the encircling darkness, like the glaring eye of someone frightened to death. The synagogue was so dark that no human shape was discernible, just one thick, clustered throng. Only after becoming accustomed to the dark could you make out heads, backs, hands grasping pillars, eyes gleaming through the grill of the women's section, and feet dangling over the balcony on the western side. An excited, hoarse voice could be heard from there, alternately angry and soothing, like an estranged family member who has come home after long travels.

Under the whip of harsh words, the crowd breathed heavily, shifting from foot to foot as they shuffled closer together forming a dense knot. They sought to hide from the lashing words that whistled overhead and coiled about the swaying wires which hung like an impending hangman's noose.

But then the exhorting voice turned gentle, comforting and calm, and the tight knot of people relaxed. They raised their heads and saw the cymbals and timbrels painted on the ceiling. The golden vessels of the Holy Temple glowed from the wall, and the Leviathan, tail in mouth, gently gazed down on them with one wide-open eye, filled with wonderment: "At last, you've lived to see the days of the Messiah, eh?"

"For two thousand years we have been in exile," the speaker continued, as if recounting a tale of once-upon-a-time, "and only now have we been redeemed, a nation like all other nations. Let us show them that we are worthy. Let all unite behind Soviet power! The bourgeoisie, the nobles, the traitors, will be destroyed" — here, once again, his voice became strident and sharp — "so that the poor will be able to survive in this world."

The tight clump of people trembled. From here and there heated, excited voices cried out. The knot burst open and like a punctured dam a flood of fervent, seething voices shouted:

"Long live...."

"Hurrah for freedom!"

"Death to traitors!"

"Betrayers!"

"Down with the Muscovites!" — swirled a cry like a poisonous snake, and was swallowed up in the surging sea of voices.

"Long live Soviet power!"

"Long live a free Poland!"

No other words could be distinguished. All the voices combined into one roar, one huge wave which swept over their heads and sent a shiver through every bone in their bodies. The crowd began to move. People stumbled against each other as they were pushed forward, into the lifeless streets which, blind and silent, reflected the enchanted shimmer of the trillions of jewels in the dark sky.

"Young men, enlist in the Red Army," a final resounding call echoed off the makeshift platform. But the speaker was drowned out by the sea of enthusiastic voices which changed from jubilant cheers into the single, distinct chorus:

"'Tis the final conflict..."

It was some time before the guards could calm the crowd and send them on their way home.

"No demonstrations are permitted at night," they warned. "We are not very far from the front lines. Don't light any fires. On your way!"

From a distant back alley came a monotonal oriental melody, sung by someone in the Bashkir regiment — "ee, ai, ai, ai ai ah." The poignant tune was like a Chassidic Shabbos-eve niggun, but it lasted only for a moment and then ceased abruptly; and with it ended the feeling of elation. A soundless fear encroached from all sides. The townspeople slipped furtively toward their laneways, thankful that their own four walls were so close at hand.

Deeply agitated, Shternberg burst into the house and threw himself, fully clothed, on the bed in the corner. He could hardly hear Chaim's fatherly scolding. "We still have a hard road ahead before we get home. You shouldn't hang around with the 'Barefoot gang.' Just take a look at yourself; you haven't enough strength to stand on your own feet. You had better get some rest," he groaned, feeling his own pain in every bone.

Shternberg stared at him as if he was a stranger, "What...?"

His heart was heavy. He was unable to grasp what was happening to him. He wished desperately to believe all that he had heard. All the anguish of his bruised body longed to believe. Naturally, he shared the crowd's jubilation, yet something troubled his thoughts.

"Is this really the awaited event? Are they really the bearers of redemption? Is it as clear and simple as all that? Can you enter a new world as simply as moving from one house to another?"

All his previous life and hopes confronted him like a wall which he could neither see through nor leap over. Everything became dim, and like a blind man he began to probe with his fingers, digging himself into the straw pallet until he fell into a heavy sleep scarred by nightmares and fright. In his ears he heard unceasingly the monotonal niggun of the Bashkirtzes, accompanied by the scurrying footsteps of frantic people who vanished into the dark lanes as if swallowed into the open gullet of a monstrous beast.

Translated from the Yiddish by
Ode Garfinkle and Mervin Butovsky

GREBLIYA STREET

GREBLIYA STREET runs straight as a ruler from the brick house at the end of the Ring Road to the short bridge alongside the water mill. From there it is only a step to the outlying district of the goyim who live near the sandpits beyond the loae hill which supplies the red, crumbly clay for all the pitted, earthen floors of the houses in the lanes.

The tumult from the Ring Road market ceases abruptly at the first porch of Grebliya Street, which, as if in self-defense, is laid out in an unswerving line with double rows of porches, one above the other. The lower porches are public; on these you can walk as far as you wish and wherever you need to go. But above them, just a few steps higher up, are separate balconies, private property, each belonging to its own house. These begin and end just where the lower porches slope a little, leaning toward the road.

It all depends on the vantage point from which you view Grebliya Street. From the lower porches it is a covered arcade — perfect as any in God's creation — all of a piece, poured from one mould. Seen from the upper porches, however, every house is separate unto itself, with its own passage to the back yard, its own drain pipes and barrel for rain-water, its own discarded utensils and junk scattered in the darkness under the balconies. These old cast-offs, unwilling to make peace with their outworn fate, boldly assert their resistance by jutting out on both sides of the open porches.

From this evidence you can immediately tell who lives above: whether a true Grebliyan, or just someone who has acquired residency through inheritance or other reasons, but clearly does not fit in with the true peers of the street — the Lazer-Isaacs and the Berra-Abbas. These are tribes of butchers, ox-herders, and horse-traders around whose front porches and

59

back yards is heard the constant din of cattle, horses, and wagons.

Town gossip, however, says that their real occupation is opening other people's stables and smuggling the animals across the border. Whether they carry out these deeds themselves or have someone else do it for them, is difficult to say. But one thing is certain, their collective nickname suits them perfectly: they are called the "gang of sitters" because they are forever "sitting" in the clink, or "sitting" on the backs of stolen horses galloping off to the far side of the border.

Under their porches are arranged long bull-whips and plain short ones, coils of rope and iron bits. Every article is marked with their insignia in red paint, just like the crest of a famous tribe. On a market day a peasant with a horse or cow to sell only has to see that mark in someone's hand and immediately he begins crossing himself and doffing his hat: "Of course I'm ready to sell. Just let the kind sir wait and I'll show him what a terrific deal this is," all the while nervously slapping the horse's rump or tugging at the teats of the cow. He knows that if he hesitates, sooner or later his barn door will stand ajar and no one will breathe a word about whose handiwork this was.

"We just can't pick up everyone," the policeman will enlighten him if he makes an accusation. "You bring me a witness who saw it himself and I'll put him in chains." Not certain who will be clapped in chains, the confused peasant leaves empty-handed.

Naturally, it is different when something happens at a nobleman's stable. Then, unfamiliar policemen appear, and together with the local constabulary, they make the rounds from one stable to another in Grebliya Street, measuring the tails and combed manes of the horses in the stalls. Usually, the search ends in one of their houses when, in mid week, the big chandeliers are lit, while from the nearby tavern a steady stream of whisky bottles and salty appetizers flows all through the night.

"You never know when you may need them," they pass on to curious neighbours. "Let an out-of-town dog lick a bone too, so he'll bark less."

But sometimes the great feast does not come to pass and only table lamps burn in their houses. Then we all know that one of them has gone to fulfill the obligation of "sitting."

II

The Berra-Abbas are just a small clan now: only Dudya, his sons and sons-in-law. All of them have red-trimmed beards with brighter flaring side-burns and large flashing eyes which pierce like slaughter knives even when they speak calmly and unhurriedly. Where Dudya finds daughters-in-law and sons-in-law who are identical to him and his children, remains his own secret. The men are tall of stature and ruddy; the women raven-haired and slender, with voices that do not reveal the hot, steaming temper seething within.

At the wedding of each son the whole town knows in advance that the new bride will be perfect from head to toe, a complexion of blood and milk, and a gait that make the porches shudder. Even more so, at a daughter's wedding, everyone anticipates Dudya's unerring choice in selecting his new family's dependents; from near or far, he always manages to find a fitting mate. The whole town is at the wedding, invited guests inside — in the big house which is just about the tallest and grandest of the entire street; the uninvited outside — beneath the high windows and on the lower porches, waiting to go along to the Shul Street where the ceremony will take place. For it has never yet happened that Dudya would break with tradition. Although he is only a horse-trader and not very observant — using oaths freely, often mocking the studious "benchwarmers," those over-zealous Chassidim who perform their extravangant preparations for prayer — yet in his own way he still has respect for those who know the small-lettered bible commentaries and he even goes to services at a Chassidic prayer-house with the "bench-warmers."

"I have to starve half-days on Shabbos," he would complain, "because they dawdle over their prayers." Yet as soon as the main "bench-warmer," Reb Shalom Becker, chides him, "Come now Dudya, it's not as bad as that," he breaks into a shamefaced smile and says, "What's wrong with eating, Reb Shalom? Can't you look into the holy books after the stew? Believe me, if it was up to me Jews would study all day long."

"So who is stopping you, my clever one?" another interjects, less good-humouredly. At this Dudya remains silent. On his tongue lies something acrid and biting, but his respect for the learned holds him back.

Only when someone forcibly treads on him does he toss

back, "Don't worry, I study in matters that concern me." Everyone then knows that they had better not provoke him further, because with that remark he alludes to the family book, a legacy from a great-grandfather, in which is recorded the annals of his proud ancestry.

This chronicle tells of his great-grandfather, the first Jew in the town, whom the old "Pauper King" had brought from a foreign place to build a settlement here. It is told of this ancestor that he traded with the independent cossacks as far as the River Bug, and still farther to the Dnieper, and that he was even admitted to the nobleman's court. Due to his efforts they were permitted to build the houses on the Jews' street as high as those of the neighbours, and they were also allowed to train and to bear arms in times of danger.

Dudya only has to mention his forefather and no one will continue the altercation. They know that if you cast doubt on his family prestige, your life hangs in the balance. Nothing arouses him to greater anger than someone questioning the truth of the story, or even whether he still has the document testifying to the family lineage. He becomes completely transformed, his ruddy cheeks and red-trimmed beard fuse into one flame, every hair bristling like a porcupine's.

Only Zonvel'le, the town fool, can allow himself to taunt Dudya about his book and his family tree, and this only during Simchas Torah celebration when Dudya becomes generous and distributes cake and whisky to the entire congregation before Hakofos — the procession of the scrolls — in the cold prayer-house.

"Live it up, everyone!" he cries, elated by feelings of well-being and expansiveness which swirl within and around him. "We have a great God! We have the holy scrolls from the shul! You can give me the last round of the processions. That's good enough for me. All the turns around the pulpit are of equal worth, friends." Weaving tipsily, he babbles on in a happy mood, surrounded by his sons and sons-in-law who hang on his every word. The women too, standing on tables and benches, are delighted that he has joined with all the shul-Jews because during the year he is never to be seen amongst them. And at a time like this who even thinks, who even recalls, that he and the sons are merely horse-dealers who, in the course of this year, as always, have fulfilled the commandment of "sitting." Even Zonvel'le, the jokester, chooses not to repeat the story that is making the rounds of the town: how once on the solemn fast-day of Tisha B'Av, when the grand-children unwittingly complained that Dudya's wife had not baked her customary blueberry buns, she answered most seriously, "Just wait, when our flesh and blood returns, God willing, we'll make up for it with a real Tish B'Av feast, with buns and other delicacies."

Now, however, it is Simchas Torah and not the deferred Tisha B'Av. And if it dawns on anyone that Dudya is, after all, a horse thief, he downs a shot of whisky, saying to himself, "So what if a Jew serves time once in a while. Who can ever know the reasons why, and anyway, who cares."

Only after innumerable glasses of whisky can Zonvel'le dare provoke Dudya, and by this time it is hard to tell whether in earnest or jest.

"Didn't you promise, Dudya, that you would come to the Hakofos with your great-grandfather's book, eh, ha? I'm curious to see what it looks like," he says slyly, fixing him with innocent eyes, "after all the fires you've had at your place."

"Shame on you for joking in front of holy things," says Dudya, pulling at Zonvel'le's pointed goatsbeard. "Do you think it's only a roll of parchment? It's real paper with leather covers. You'll see it yet." He smiles drunkenly. "Don't worry, my grandfather preserved it well. A wonderful person was my grandfather, a wonderful man, you hear? All the village peasants from here to the River Bug, trembled before him."

Had it not been time to recite the opening prayer, he undoubtedly would have rambled on about his grandfather, and told how he had built the original prayer-house which burnt down in the time of the evil edicts of Chmelnitzki the destroyer — may his name be erased. After the devastation, only the eastern wall of the prayer house remained standing, so the desecrators nailed the wooden troughs for their horses to the exposed beams, exactly behind the place where the Holy Ark had stood. Yet didn't all their starving nags catch the sleeping sickness that same night? And when gradfather and his band attacked them before daybreak, ambushing them by the waters of the River Vuhl, not a single one of them remained alive. "That was a real grandfather!"

His eyes shine boastfully as he strides to his seat against the eastern wall, accompanied by his sons and sons-in-law. It takes some time before he sits down. He looks around, observing his neighbours who sit waiting for the cantor to begin. He doesn't open his mouth again, but his bearing proudly declares, "Zaide, we are here!"

Impatiently, he sits the long while until his turn comes at Hakofos. Then he lets loose, singing even louder than the cantor, while the whole tribe of Berra-Abbas joins in: "Saviour of the poor, redeem us!" This is their Hakofah and no one dares accompany them around the pulpit; not at least, since that one time when the Lazer-Isaac clan, being drunk, pretended to forget and joined their procession. Soon, candle-holders and lecterns began to fly; blood ran all the way from the shul to Grebliya Street.

All during the procession around the cantor's pulpit, Dudya constantly looks behind to see, first of all, whether anyone has pushed in amongst them, but more importantly, to demonstrate to his offspring the proper way to embrace the Torah Scroll with the right hand, while, with the left, holding the open prayer book. The sons don't take their eyes from him, but they have something else on their minds. They want to discover whether he happens to be carrying the Zaide Book under his arm. He is always talking about the book, and even tells them that he takes it along to every important occasion but none of them has yet seen it. When the older son, Yosha — who considers himself a bit of a scholar — presses him for information about the book, Dudya abruptly cuts him off: "When the time comes, you'll know everything. When it is necessary, I take it with me. That was Zaide's way, so we do the same thing. We'll know when the time comes to pass it on to the eldest son. Is that clear?"

After that scolding, there are no further questions. But everyone knows that at all important family gatherings, and in preparation for a big transaction, he will ponder over the family book which is locked in an old wooden chest mounted on wheels, and bound with iron hoops. The chest stands in his bedroom and the key is not entrusted even to his own wife.

Everyone knows that when he leads a child to the marriage canopy the book accompanies the bride, serving as a protective charm for passing the small haunted garden in front of the shul, where, it is told, lie the bride and groom who were pitilessly slaughtered by the Haidamik cossacks as they stood under the canopy. But Dudya hides the book so well within the pleats of the bride's crinoline, that no one can even notice it and, since he alone accompanies the bride, it might be that he has stuffed it into the wide pockets of his knee-length coat. No one dares question him. The entire town stands in amazement at how Dudya has, once again, found a choice son-in-law; every inch a Berra-Abba, as if born into the tribe. The balcony shakes beneath the groom, while, a little behind, Dudya leads his daughter, wrapt in shawls which dazzle the eye. The veil, another heirloom in the family for generations, a little worn but stiffly starched, can barely cover the braids of the bride's thick black hair, which Dudya tries to hide from the eyes of the congregation, and which the hair dresser, imported from "little Paris", has spent all day trying to disguise as a wig. In the same way, they had evaded the required marriage rituals by paying the mikva attendant for both the ceremonial immersion and the hair-cutting, although in truth, she only symbolically snipped off a tip of the braid which Dudya himself will hide in the pages of his book, the same book held by the first Berra-Abba when he lay breathless in the sands by the river bank with a small band of Jews, ready to resist Chmelnitzki's marauders who had overrun all the surrounding woods and fields.

Translated from the Yiddish by
Ode Garfinkle and Mervin Butovsky

THEY CALLED HIM HUNYA

DESPITE the raging snow-storm and bitter frost about twenty people came to Hunya's funeral. One by one, breathlessly, they stamped into the dimly-lit mortuary. Without glancing about to see who was there, they chose their seats at the rear or centre benches, careful to distance themselves from their neighbours. They sat with lowered heads, bundled up, rigid with cold. Only when the door sprang open admitting a gust of icy wind, did they permit themselves mutely to observe the newcomer, following him to the bench, where, just as they had, he took his seat huddled in a wet overcoat, leaving a space between himself and others.

It seemed as if they were afraid of something and wished to conceal it from a stranger's eye, yet all the eyes here were familiar; they had known each other for years. They seemed to shuffle forward with uncertain steps, while glancing sideways, in order to measure which seat would not be considered too far back yet close enough to the unoccupied front pews. These formed a grey, desolate barrier between the assembled mourners and the black coffin which hovered like an elongated shadow over the narrow metal stand alongside the dais which was equipped with lecterns, projecting microphones, and two flickering candles. A six-branched candelabra threw fragments of light into the gloom, piercing the darkened corner where, forlorn and remote from each other, sat the only son and younger brother of the dead man. The aura surrounding the casket was like a mysterious circle repelling the furtive glances which sought to reach it over the barren space.

An unseen yoke of guilt seemed to press on the spirit of the mourners, driving them apart. Sitting amidst old friends they could not face one another, nor speak to a neighbour. Not one of them could have traced the source of the guilt, yet they experienced a haunting oppression when they met the sidelong glances of their friends. Instinctively they recoiled, distancing themselves still further from the casket and the desolate family.

For many years most of them had lost touch with Hunya, had not even troubled to enquire after him. When someone casually mentioned his name — telling of his recovery from earlier losses, how he had set up a small furrier's shop somewhere in a remote alley far from the Jewish neighbour-hood — then they had listened with open curiosity and shaken their heads. And when the informant added: "He seems to be getting along. For one thing he drops into the Yiddish school from time to time and leaves a generous donation for the annual campaign, and he also sends contributions to the 'Exploration Fund' for a new Jewish territory..." at this point, hearing these details, they wanted more.

"That is the only cause he still believes in, he told me. However, his donations are given on the condition that they be anonymous, and the receipts sent to his only son being raised by his mother's distant relatives. That family can't bear to hear Hunya's name mentioned. When they receive anything from him they recoil as if touched by a snake and the gift is immediately returned with a note: let him keep it and may he choke on it."

Hearing this, the listeners allow themselves a show of sympathy: "He is to be pitied, despite everything. Do you see him often?"

That is where things stood. It never occurred to any of them to try to meet him, to draw him back to the group. Even when they learned from the Yiddish newspaper — this was several years later — that someone had been awarded a prize for a glossary of Yiddish terms used in the fur trade, a submission without the compiler's name and address, and people immedi-ately ascribed that work to him — even then only one of them made the effort to locate him. Later, he reported that Hunya's entire factory consisted of a single room where he worked and lived alone. He only went out for his weekly vegetarian needs or to deliver his piece-work. When reproached for not signing his name and address to the manuscript, he answered: "A person should leave behind only the fruit of his knowledge, that which he knows better than anyone else. What has his name to do with anything?"

"A new recluse! Suddenly, he's become a saint!" retorted his former friends, their scorn combined with grudging respect.

"It looks like the case of someone trying to expiate a sin," was the way the visitor summed up his impressions.

At that, the old antipathy surfaced openly: "He has plenty to atone for."

"For himself alone, he told me he needs little. Some vegetables, bread, and salt, are enough. His son Moishele is already independent — an accomplished engineer — able to manage his own affairs. What troubled him most was really us — our group — how we allowed ourselves to be deceived, the way we clung to our community leaders while they continued to lie and throw sand in our eyes, which we blindly accepted as pure gold. Our world was doomed and no one really cared. We thought only of ourselves. Already there was no one with whom to exchange an honest Yiddish word."

"Let him keep his muddled thoughts to himself and not beat his breast on another's heart." After that, his name was no longer mentioned and recollections of him were consciously avoided.

What could explain their presence here now? Why, after reading the short obituary notice, had they ventured out on a stormy, forbidding day to pay their final respects? Sitting apart, like strangers, a remorseless question gnawed at their hearts: Once, you thought you knew a person whom you later deliberately cast aside. Unexpectedly, you learn that he is gone forever and that irreversible act shocks you into the realization that you never really knew him. All your earlier assumptions about him clarify nothing.

As soon as the notice appeared in the newspaper, some telephones in the city began to ring anxiously, and agitated voices asked, "Have you heard?"

"Really, is that a fact, when, how?"

"Someone must be found to say a few words, despite everything. But why me? Did I really know him?"

Who knew him any better?

It was far into the night when his brother finally persuaded one of the group to say the few parting words, and then only after resorting to harsh reproaches, spoken with dulled bitterness.

"Does it seem right to you that he be so humiliated? That he be cast off like a rag, like a broken pot? Whatever you thought of him, he was a human being, your own friend. Believe me, the family has better grounds for complaint than any you might claim, but how can you treat another person this way? His son doesn't want any rabbi in attendance, and rightly so. What did he have to do with rabbis? Remember, he was always one of yours. Every bit of humanity that he did have was invested entirely in your group and your beliefs. Does that mean nothing to you now?"

Sitting alone in a corner, he anxiously awaits the moment when he must speak, when he must find words for the impenetrable mystery. *Only now are you willing to confront the truth, yet still fear the consequences of your thought. Was it because in refusing to learn the truth about him — relying instead on condemnation and rejection — you had contributed to his lifelong homelessness, to his miserable death, somewhere alone in a hovel with a curse on his lips for everything and everyone. And when you come to think of it for a moment, isn't it the same with each and every one of us? What do I know about them; what do they know about me?* Before his eyes, in a blur, the disconsolate glances of each of the huddled ones merged.

Maybe he should begin by recounting the strange discussion he had with Hunya some days ago when something he couldn't name prompted him to telephone and make enquiries. As soon as Hunya recognized his voice, he actually gasped in wonder: "Really? Only to find out how I'm doing? It can't be..." his rasping voice spoke in disbelief, "have I made the dreadful mistake of thinking no one cared whether or not I am still alive. Too bad that I've found out so late...." He wasn't certain whether Hunya was merely being playfully sarcastic or speaking out of a deep resentment against them all. "At least there is one pious man in Sodom...." Nevertheless, Hunya didn't cut him off and continued speaking as if he wanted to pour out his heart. "I've already endured my allotted days. The game ends in checkmate."

"Do we ever learn anything from the moves of the game?" This slipped out involuntarily, as in the old days, when he used to spar with Hunya at the chess tables in the club.

"If only I could understand even a little, everything might have been different."

Hunya then abruptly broke off the talk, but almost seemed

to plead that he come to see him. This he never managed.

Is that how we should begin the words of farewell? What would it explain? Would it add anything to what they already knew? For it was common knowledge that Hunya had arrived here with a reputation for community work, bringing with him from the old country a fanatic's devotion for Yiddish language and culture as well as an abrasive distrust for anyone holding opinions that differed from his own. He actually quivered in anger when someone spoke a sympathetic word for the religious tradition. Nor did he spare those who invested all their hopes in the struggle for social justice, or in the nationalistic rebuilding of Eretz Yisroel.

"It's only delusion, a case of being misled," he would exclaim fiercely, proceeding to insult his opponents with the sharpest epithets. "I trust no one in this brutish world. They fool us with their fancy talk which only masks their real intentions. This has already cost us rivers of blood and more will yet be demanded because we allow ourselves to be betrayed by alien illusions."

Often carried away by anger, such discussions came close to blows.

"Not a single territory, but many territories. That's our need. Even when history permits us to play with our own deck of cards, it's simply madness to bet everything on a single card. In this case we should listen to our leader, because, as we all know, Palestine is a shimmering, jewelled table coveted by thieving hands from ancient times until today."

In turn, he wasn't spared their insults and name-calling, which pierced to the seventh rib. Some stopped talking to him and demanded his expulsion from the circle. However, the majority maintained that the group was founded principally to promote Yiddish cultural activities and to enrich their personal lives, so it behoved them to be tolerant of diverse opinions, especially, as in this case, if it concerned one of their most active members. They knew that for his convictions he was prepared, when he undertook a project, to do more than anyone else — even when he had to act alone.

His dogged convictions were most evident during and immediately following the war years when he immersed himself totally, night and day, in work for the "Committee for War Victims," collecting money and packing food parcels to be

71

sent to the displaced-persons camps and individuals whose addresses had reached them through various channels. In every parcel he, like the others, placed a note asking the recipient for any scraps of information about members of his family. But here too, something was odd. Unlike the others who used a standard style for their notes and usually showed them to one another to assure the legibility of the handwriting, he never allowed anyone to see his messages. Yet they knew, and whispered to each other in secret, that each of his notes was signed with a different name, disguising the sender's identity. From these notes they pieced together that he was enquiring about his large family, one of considerable importance in his town. There was also a veiled reference to some event — an event which had appalled the entire region — involving a member of that family. Naturally, our curiosity swelled, but no one wanted to admit that we were spying on him.

We also knew that he was about to lose his "rag shop" — his mocking term for his workplace. He almost completely abandoned his business as soon as he learned that one of his brothers, whom he hardly knew (having left home when the brother was still a child) had been located in a displaced-persons camp somewhere in Germany. He chased from office to office and then disappeared for several weeks, returning with a young man who bore some physical resemblance to him, yet couldn't have been more different in his conduct with other people. The younger brother was open-hearted and — in contrast to Hunya — enthusiastically recounted incidents from his past; the only exception being any reference to the time when Hunya would still have lived at home. At such moments he would stop abruptly, sensing Hunya's irritation and glowering face. Hunya arranged work for his brother and his wife in a fur factory, looking after their needs to the limit of his means. From that time he would seldom be found at home. Among the group it was whispered that his sick wife and only child were destitute. Neighbours revealed that his miserliness begrudged his own family food for the table and denied them the everyday necessities.

"After the catastrophe over there, we can't afford to indulge ourselves," he deliberately explained to the neighbour who accosted him one night on the balcony near his doorway.

"But surely she must be taken to a doctor," the neighbour

protested.

"How come you know everything?" he stared at her at length and growled, "they suffered infinitely more over there." He then slipped into the house and was not seen for the next few days.

"There isn't a decent sheet in the house, nor an extra pot," the neighbours appealed to some members of the group. We were stunned in disbelief, since, when others were in need, his generosity was always unstinting. We all assumed that this was within his means and praised him for his kindness.

"Who could have known that all his public charity and sympathy for others turned to rage and cruelty when it came to his own family. Who can comprehend such behaviour?" So aid was secretly given his wife and child, but not one of us dared raise the subject with him.

It seemed as if a barrier had always existed between him and the group ever since that first time when he appeared at a gathering and introduced himself in an odd outspoken way:

"They call me Hunya," he said extending a strongly calloused hand with blackened fingers, "for my beliefs I'm prepared to put my neck on the block."

He didn't utter another word that evening, yet everyone sensed his attentiveness and realized that he would be heard from again. Quite naturally, he was invited to attend the meetings more often, and indeed, he did show up. Only now are incidents recalled which, at that time, had not aroused the least attention. After all, who has the time or patience to dig into the reasons for someone's belonging to a cultural group: why he joins, becomes a part of it, and then suddenly withdraws, as if he had never belonged. Now, when it was all over, everyone felt that Hunya had made efforts to become close, to join in all their activities, to be one with them. Yet, in truth, he remained estranged and distant. He was seldom invited to anyone's house, and no one remembered entering his home. Usually, the blame was attributed to his wife who was considered to be strangely silent and obviously stuck-up (at least that's what we thought). She never looked a person straight in the eye. She seemed to keep herself hidden and acted like a frightened hen in company — on those rare occasions when she condescended to come to a meeting. At other times she acted like a spoiled only-child: "You may look at me, but don't touch. I have nothing in common with you."

"She really thinks she's something special," they gossiped, and then ignored her. Even when she became sick, malicious tongues interpreted this as a mere pretense, pitying him for having to put up with her, accusing her of preventing any closeness to him.

"In truth, aside from his fanaticism, he could always be counted on. Everyone acknowledges that you never left his place empty-handed. But, you had to approach him only at his shop. He really has no home...."

How were they to know what torment consumes a person, and what kind of hell he bears within him. But this was revealed only much, much later.

The fact that people addressed him by his first name was no sign of familiarity. They hardly knew his family name, which he seldom mentioned, and then, with his usual irony: "There is nothing to boast about. Just call me Hunya."

The manner in which he said this, combined with the nervous, mocking smile which played over his long, bony, pointed face, signalled that this was not his real name either, but some sort of nickname whose origin he alone knew. Since the group included others who for various reasons had taken fictitious names, it was assumed that "Hunya" was leftover from those former days when he had to erase the family name from memory. Sometimes, when he was in high spirits and became almost intimate with one of the group, he would suddenly say: "You know — I almost said y'know — as we used to pronounce it back home — I'm so used to my single name that I hardly remember my original ones, especially the family name, it barely exists for me. When I need to sign an official document I have to strain to remember, and the shadow of those memories leaves a bitter taste in my mouth."

After such disclosures, the listener naturally tried to pry a bit more out of him, but he immediately withdrew behind a concealed barrier: "Why dig up the yesterdays, it's all nonsense."

Even Hunya's son came to know his family name only when he enrolled in school. Until then, he had simply heard the name Hunya used by his mother and the neighbours who cared for them when the mother was bed-ridden. So he called him Hunya too when he spoke about him in his absence, just as he did on those rare evenings when Hunya remained at home, and the boy would cuddle up to him before sleep and listen to fantastic stories about faraway lands inhabited by strange people who were constantly hungry, who lived in clay huts with thatched roofs.

One of the bedtime stories was about a father so cruel that he didn't deserve to be called father; he never smiled and never allowed his children to raise their heads or do what they wished. So he came to a terrible end. All his children deserted him and from that time refused to speak his name. The story did not always have the same ending. Sometimes, it concluded when one of the children, in a great rage, did something so dreadful to the cruel father, that a calamity befell the entire family. Once, when the evening's tale was nearly over and the child was overwhelmed with pity for the mistreated children, he tremblingly drew closer to Hunya and said, "Hunya is a good father; isn't he good?" With a shudder, Hunya hastily detached himself from the child's arms and in a voice unfamiliar to his son, rasped: "I am" — he began, then stopped to swallow as if choking. He snatched up the child and laid him on the bed: "Moishele, you must always call me Hunya!" That stern entreaty and distraught look, remained with the child forever.

The child. now grown up, sits in a corner as hunched and frightened as he was then, staring about confused and troubled.

"Oi, Hunya, Hunya," — he seems to hear his uncle's sobs from the other end of the bench where he sits lost in himself. He ought to move closer to him. Who else does he have now? Moving closer to his uncle might possibly dissolve the frozen, clotted resentment which blocks out the image of his father, of Hunya. *Now he must know everything.* He begins to move, but actually finds himself further away from him. Out of the cold a sharp gnawing feeling forces him back. When his uncle came from Europe after the great catastrophe, the last bit of affection which Hunya had shown for his sick mother also vanished. Everything was done for his uncle's family, while for his mother Hunya reckoned every single cent, and gradually stopped coming home at all. If it hadn't been for the neighbours and his mother's distant relatives, who helped them without his knowledge, they simply would have died of hunger and cold.

Out of that forbidding past, emerges a cheerless Sunday

afternoon. His uncle came to take him to his house. "It's Chanukah, so you'll come and play with the children. Here's a dreidle." Hunya was there, in a happy mood. He distributed Chanukah gelt and let the children call him uncle, rewarding them with a kiss. When he attempted the same, Hunya shook him off in anger, "Have you already forgotten my name?"

He never went there again, nor did his uncle ever visit them. The tears he shed on the way home are still freezing in his half-closed eyes.

Later, when the uncle had completely estranged himself from Hunya, the reason was never made clear to him. "A family quarrel," his mother began to explain to him. "Hunya had thought that by saving his brother he would atone the youthful deed against his own father — a 'saint' just like him. But the uncle is kneaded of the same dough as Hunya, and can't forgive him, so both continue to pay for it. This has darkened our lives." She refused to speak about it further. "You're better off not knowing. In any case you're not like them and should have as little to do with them as possible. I have suffered enough from them." After that, she refused to answer his questions.

What had he done? Why had he unleashed his terrible rage on us?

"Oi Hunya, Hunya," his uncle's sobs reached him again in the muffled silence of the funeral parlour, now fused with the choked cries of his sick mother emerging out of a distant recess of the past. It is a late winter night when the house had not been heated for days. Shivering from cold and hunger, he lies huddled under the ragged comforter from which tufts of cotton creep into his mouth.

He hears Hunya's embittered, hoarse voice. "You dazzled me with your family status, and your persuasive tongue deceived me. Some family! Only when I came here did I begin to understand what you had done to me. What could a naive young man have known then. I thought I was getting ready to serve Progress and Revolution. It was all your fault. You have to pay for it...."

Only now does he begin to sense the thrust of that pitiless accusation. The meaning that had eluded him throughout childhood suddenly seems to emerge before him as if someone had revealed its hidden significance.

"But why should the child suffer for this?" His mother's voice pierces the darkness surrounding his bed, as it now broke through the encrusted pain.

"I alone will pay for it," was Hunya's dejected reply.

"And you have plenty to pay for, you monster. For what you did over there, and what you've done to us. Do you think people are blind? Everyone knows, and they'll be told everything. You are beyond forgiveness." Then the voice fades, becoming inaudible.

Only his father's voice continues to reach him through the gloom: "Certainly I'll pay for it, I'll pay for it...."

Looking up at the black casket and the nearly empty benches which extend far back into the hall, he cannot seem to determine where he is. He finds it impossible to locate the source of the images and voices which have just enthralled him. They remain beyond recall, caught in the irretrievable past.

Nor can he grasp why, suddenly, a week ago, he had flown all the way from South Africa where he now lives, and where he thought he had completely erased all this. Out of nowhere, in the midst of his preoccupation with a new project which completely absorbed him, he was overwhelmed by a strange uneasiness and, defenselessly, transported back to those dark times. After so many years of estrangement he found himself once again standing with Hunya on a rainy autumn day at the corner of some back-alley, shivering beneath the needle-sharp pellets of freezing rain. This was his last meeting before departure. A shrunken, saddened Hunya tried to explain something to him which he could barely comprehend.

"I want you to know" — he swallowed his words hastily — "who knows if we will ever see each other again, Moishele. Maybe it's better this way, that you should forget everything here." He stretched out his hand as if to embrace him, then quickly snatched it back. "But, you should know that a person instinctively wants to recapture the role of a father, or a grandfather. At first I didn't want that for myself, and then discovered that it was too late for me."

As suddenly and mysteriously as that image and voice had appeared, it seemed to dissolve, leaving an anxious disquiet and unspeakable heartfelt longing. He could no longer concentrate on his work as he had done earlier. Both in his waking hours and restless sleep, some unfulfilled demand plagued him: "I should return, maybe I will discover something." He couldn't make clear to himself why he was suddenly impelled to know, but all his senses pressed him to postpone the trip no longer. He had to see his father again, with his own eyes.

Seated in the airplane, everything remained confused and he was beseiged by questions: *Why is he actually returning and for whom?* Some years earlier he had seen to it that his mother's grave would be cared for. With that act he had completely blocked Hunya out of his memory. It had already become difficult to recall his actual features. Frequently, he had begun to doubt whether he had even known anyone like that. And if he sometimes saw someone who resembled his father, it seemed like a shadow of a forgotten dream which merged into oblivion without leaving a trace of attachment, certainly nothing recognizable as a son's feelings for a father. He had never tasted father-love and even the word "father" had been heard from other children; never once had he uttered the word. What clung to his memory was an echo of the name "Hunya," which appeared and disappeared from the house leaving behind reverberations of anguished pain. Sometimes this shadow-name personified itself, becoming tall and bony, with a twisted smile on its angular face. The thin hands stretched out with longing, embraced him for a moment, then, with a shudder, dropped the crying boy on his bed.

"He'll pay for everything he's done," his mother's lips trembled as she wiped away his tears. "Forget him, my child. Wipe out his memory, as if he never existed."

It was only after he began school that he would sometimes see Hunya standing in the schoolyard waiting for him with some sweets, asking how he was getting along and whether he was making progress in his studies. From the signs of unmistakable friendliness displayed toward the teachers, he saw that they considered Hunya one of them. They responded warmly to Hunya and he found this unbelievable, impossible to grasp.

Why does he have a smile for everyone, except us? This thought always left an acrid bitter taste on his tongue which could be spit out only when he moved away from him, but never put into words. In the same way he stifled the urge to confront his teachers: why do they speak so readily to him, politely answering questions about his son's progress and behaviour.

Don't they realize the truth?

When he saw Hunya walking in his direction in the schoolyard his immediate reaction was to avoid him and escape back into the classroom, but something in Hunya's eyes riveted him to the spot. Yet, strangely, after standing close to each other for a few moments, he often felt saddened when the bell called him back to the classroom. Feelings that he had not managed to express seemed on the verge of violent eruption. The sound of the bell blocked them deep in his throat. He gagged on its congealed bitterness and could only find relief by spitting out the revolting aftertaste. Once, a teacher caught him and he was immediately taken out of line and given a harsh reprimand. "That's disgusting. If only your father would have seen that...." The teacher was indignant; the children teased, "His father brings him such candies that burn the tongue."

Even now, while all these moments flash by with kaleidoscopic speed, like shards of memory continuously revealed then erased, he feels the same bitterness on his tongue, a bitterness beyond the reach of words. And something else still gnaws at him: *What did you actually do, Hunya? How were you so cruelly betrayed, and by whom?*

He stands up suddenly as if stupefied. His eyes confusedly take in the flickering candles and the black casket which seems to embody his mother's sickly voice which had remained fixed in his mind since his final visit to the Hospital of Hope.

"I am at peace now, Moishele, happy that you saved yourself," she muttered through a half-paralyzed mouth. He could hardly grasp the meaning of her words. "Kind people took care of you when you were abandoned by our family. Try not to condemn us, my son...." She made an anguished effort to stretch out her arms but was abruptly pitched back on the bed where she lay glaring with astonishment into the unknown void. For an instant her twisted mouth straightened, and then a disquieting yellow pallor began to stain the fallen cheeks and sharp, bony chin.

Quivering with fear, he hears the sound of his own cry, "Ma!" As the surging foam seeped down the corners of her mouth, his entire being sensed the distant past reverberate like a liberating chord, shimmering in the unsteady light above the coffin.

He feels submerged in that unreal chord which speaks to

him distinctly: "You see, I have borne my fate." With that, the frost that bound him seemed to dissolve.

All parts of his body seem unified. All his senses are open and keen. In the space of a second, events, people, places, flash by. He feels himself dispersed through all time, through all space. In overlapping, simultaneous waves he hears his uncle's sobs, the unintelligible sounds muttered from his mother's frothy lips, and Hunya's hoarse voice a rapid staccato, plunging on breathlessly.

He appears before him as he found him a few days ago, shrunken, lying prone on his iron bed in the near-empty room. When Hunya caught sight of him on his doorstep carrying the bags of groceries which he had bought on his uncle's advice, he ironically upbraided him for such delicacies: "Who do you think I am, your grandfather Isaac who expected to be served a lavish feast?" With that, he even strained to smile.

"But it is good that you have come in time ... Moishele."

As always the hoarse voice both soothed and disturbed him. His prepared speech, laden with accusations, caught in his throat.

"I was about to send for you ... not because I need something from you. I realize it is too late for that. I only want you to know that I deceived myself into believing that I could correct one injustice by committing an even greater one. Neither can I bring myself to ask forgiveness just as I can't expect anyone else to ask it of me. It is now clear to me that of all creatures on earth, man alone brings ruin on his own kind. Not because of hunger, no: he convinces himself that he acts in the name of an ideal, a holy belief for which the world was created. The greatest of evils we reserve for those we hold dearest, then we destroy ourselves. We become loathsome in our own eyes...."

More rapidly now, he began to swallow his words and indicated with his hand that he was not to be interrupted.

"I committed a grievous sin against you and your mother. I didn't realize until it was too late that all a man needs is the sense to warm himself in the sun, to say a word of praise for work well done, to take pleasure in raising children and grandchildren."

With that, he choked and began to stammer. His eyes held Moishele's unwaveringly.

"Now I know that someone who withholds his affections from his nearest, his dearest, is unworthy..." he raised himself abruptly, then fell back drained.

"You see Moishele, how we inflict punishment on ourselves."

Through the icy fastness the long-rejected cry, "Oi Tateh!" flowed in a warm, soothing flood of tears.

"Maybe we could recite a chapter of Psalms?"

"Absolutely not! He wasn't a believer." His uncle's distant voice in argument with the shammes reaches him as if muffled by a curtain.

"But the mourner's ritual cut must be made!"

The shammes stands before him, knife extended. "And what was your father called?"

"Nachman, son of Huna Ze'ev," interjects the uncle, holding his outstretched tie to the shammes' knife. His eyes widen in astonishment when he hears Moishele's words, spoken in a melancholy whisper, slowly weighing every syllable as if wanting to savour the taste of each word as it accompanies the knife's rhythmic sundering, "No, they called him Hunya! Hunya is what they called my father."

Translated from the Yiddish by
Ode Garfinkle and Mervin Butovsky

THAT FIRST MORNING

"THERE IS no need to carry it about with you here," said Uncle Chaim smiling, and with discernible pride in his voice he plucked away the passport which Shternberg was about to place in his breast pocket, just as he had always done in earlier years, before he left his house.

"No one will ask to see it here and no one cares who you are or where you are going. You only need to remember your address so you can find your way home. Leave the passport with your papers, together with your landing card; it will be required only when you want to become a citizen. Until then, as long as you have a house to live in you're a resident, and no one has the right to stop you and ask you questions. Here — that's the kind of country it is — as long as you don't bother anyone it is no one's business who you are," said the slim blond uncle in an almost celebratory manner as he stretched out his hand and with warm-hearted affection accompanied him from the house.

"May the occasion of your first walk be blessed. I would like to go along with you this first time, especially since it is a rare sun-filled day. Soon it will begin to grow so wild with snow storms that you won't be able to stick your nose outdoors. But I have to rush back to the store; the little chicks can't chirp without their boss. Your aunt thinks you're still a small-towner who is frightened of tall buildings and long streets, but I know my customers and I'm sure you can take care of yourself. Still, don't tell her that I let you go out alone; by the time she gets back in the late afternoon you will have returned. It's hard to get lost here. The streets are straight in all directions. For the first time don't go too far, and take care to look about before you cross the street, they drive like the devils here — everyone in a great hurry. You'll soon see for yourself;

even while walking on the sidewalk, pay attention to the traffic on the street."

Of all his uncle's words, what stayed in Shternberg's mind was, "No one here cares who you are." Somehow this gladdened him yet at the same time left an empty feeling tinged with loneliness.

Amidst the bustling tumult of the main street that feeling intensified. Even when he stood at the entrance to a shop no one looked at him or asked if he wanted anything. Whenever he saw a policeman he would from long habit touch his breast pocket and a helpless fear twinged his heart when he felt its emptiness. A well-groomed, clean-shaven policeman passed him, quietly playing with his brown billy-stick as if silently counting the steps. Only after he had passed did the lump in Shternberg's throat dissolve. A warm feeling of security seemed to grow out of the unfamiliar street noises, the half-opened doors of the shops, and the steep grey stairs in the side alleys which, at the top, leaned against the high brown and red brick walls as if protruding from the windows while clinging with their last strength to the cracked sidewalks beneath.

Suddenly he was stunned — tears actually came to his eyes — when at the corner of the street he saw a policeman encircled by children who gaily chattered to him, and then, before he knew it, one was perched on the policeman's shoulder, a second under his arm, while the smallest was tucked against his heart as he carried them across the street. The sight of children waving joyfully at the smiling policeman so moved him that all the frightful stories of his childhood and his own experience of terror with gendarmes on the other side of the ocean melted into a sense of well-being. Unthinkingly, he began to chatter along with the children, repeating their few comprehensible words, "Thank you, Tom!" Within him there welled up his uncle's proud tone: "That's the kind of country it is!" He had the sensation that each step he took caressed the black asphalt with a refrain: "How good, how good and pleasing it is in this country."

Added to this, the openings in the middle of the row houses, which gave the appearance of one long wall divided by the sloping stairs, began to remind him of familiar alleys. The narrow back-yards to which they led were stacked with scrap iron or lumber; within them trudged men with wind-carved faces clad in heavy fur-lined winter coats. They called to one another in an odd dialect, a mixture of words which seemed like guttural Yiddish combined with a slurred Ukrainian, spiced with incomprehensible swallowed sounds in a language he thought he had heard on the boat but which he failed to understand at all. The whole scene transmitted a deep familiarity, permeated with old-country odours. It seemed that he had been here once before, but he could not recall the time. If only he could knock at a door and enter, he was sure he would remember.

An elderly woman hurried by, hidden in heavy winter wrappings with a black shawl covering her head and shoulders. He has already seen her somewhere, shabby-looking, carrying a basket full of giblets, several loaves of bread and other foodstuffs which diminished as she hobbled from house to house in her ungainly manner. In these alleys where poverty dwelt he could almost call her by name and if the curved steep wooden steps were swept away he would even know who lived in these houses and who awaited her arrival. Today is Thursday and in her basket she brings the preparations for Shabbos.

An angry voice from the highest window suddenly broke the spell of the dancing bounce of her basket, "You fool, you shlimazl, what will you do with it, where will you keep it and for what? All he does is drag together junk from who knows where!" A wrinkled face framed by a thin red kerchief shouted at a short man in a ragged grey jacket belted with a rope. Into the yard he rolled a wooden barrel and a rubber tire which repeatedly collided against the stairs. Triply bent over, he stumbled, breathing heavily, "Stop already! It's worth a whole dollar!"

A compelling curiosity to enter one of the houses and make himself at home drew Shternberg to every door. But he was deterred by the boisterous playing of a group of children right under the stairs. Vapours rose from their overheated bodies as they gripped bent sticks in their outstretched red and blue hands, chasing a flat, round disc which was always getting caught under the stairs or being arrested by the cracks of the broken sidewalk. Sweat poured down their reddened foreheads leaving white rivulets on their soiled faces. The players seemed indifferent to this, so engrossed were they in anticipating the exact moment when the disc would come within range, unobstructed by the stairs or the cracks. In the middle of the street, tired birds searching for crumbs of food in the horse manure, hopped back and with a flutter rescued themselves by flying up to the high snowy ledges near the roof tops of the identical row-houses, locked into one another as if shaped by the same mold. Only then did he notice that as far as the eye could see not a single tree could be found on the whole street.

"Where do the birds have their nests?" it suddenly dawned on him to ask a boy racing by.

"What?" The small boy opened a pair of questioning eyes and called out, "Greenhorn!"

That this term was intended as an insult, Shternberg had already learned from a passenger on board ship who was on his way to Canada for the second time. Now, as the epithet suddenly struck him and quickly slid by along with the impatient mocking grimace of the excited boy, it sounded more like pity for someone, ostensibly an adult who doesn't even know the rules of the game in which a bystander should not presume to interfere.

The scurrying of the game abruptly ended in the midst of its urgency when a protracted sad niggun resounded from the corner of the street. The gravelly, monotonal melody rose from a run-down horse and wagon which rolled toward him step by step, stopping whenever the niggun was obscured by the noise of a window opened and shut again, then rolled on for another few paces until a coarse voice rang out from the wagon: "I pay cash! I buy junk! Gold for rags!" When no door or window opened, the tuneful cry rolled on in the same monotone, to the rhythmic squeaking of the wagon: "I-pa-a-y ca-a-sh!"

The excited youngsters rushed toward the wagon in one throng, their bent sticks held high, their shouts filling the street with sound, mimicking the pedlar's niggun with cheerful cries, "Gold for ra-a-a-gs!" The horse stopped and uttered an odd, peculiar neigh as if in recognition, answering them by twisting its head from side to side and flicking its tail back and forth. The wagon rolled a little further and, with a loud squeak, came to a stop. Even the heap of rumpled mattresses with extruding rusty springs shook, it seemed, with knowing familiarity toward the cluster of children. They surrounded the wagon yet kept their distance beyond the range of the whip in the hands of the thin, wiry pedlar. He sat on the hard wagon-seat in a crumpled stiff fedora, as if he were part of the greasy stovepipe extending from the black oven-heater on which he leaned.

"High, high,
Smoke reach the sky,
Grab an alley-cat
By the thigh."

The children mocked his drawn-out niggun and poked their sticks into the pile of junk — "I buy everything, hip, hip!" — then dashed away in all directions when the whip's crack awakened the sleepy street.

"Get away you ruffians! Don't touch the goods!" the pedlar shouted, jumping from the wagon. "Isn't it enough that the other boys don't let me ride through in peace." His outburst sounded more like a plea than a cry of anger. "May you never come to my bitter fate. Go find yourselves better playthings." He didn't make the slightest effort to pursue the children, just leaned against the wagon, threw his head back expertly and cast a squinted glance at the windows on both sides of the street. From a few open windows angry mothers called down to their children in dismay, "What do you want from the poor man? I'll tell your father and you'll get it!"

Taking advantage of the open windows the pedlar sang out, "Gold for rags!" in the highest register, which silenced both children and mothers. In a moment he rushed to one of the curved staircases and, in a short while, slipped down with another sack of rags for his loaded wagon.

Satisfied with himself, the ragman made the street resound once more to the crack of his whip. The horse began to trot along, turning its head back toward the children who were immersed again in chasing the round disc, no longer attentive to the horse and wagon from which only a stiff fedora could be seen and a half-drowsy tremulous monotone heard, fading further and further down the empty street.

Translated from the Yiddish by
Ode Garfinkle and Mervin Butovsky

AFTERWORD

THE HISTORY of Yiddish literature in Canada is of brief duration yet, in concert with other bodies of modern Jewish writing, it conveys the wrenching dislocations and painful rebirth which mark the immigrant experience. The language and literature of East European Jewry was brought to Canada by an immigrant generation uprooted from their countries of origin: Poland, Ukraine, Lithuania or Rumania. The Canadian Jewish community was substantially formed by these migrants who arrived during the four decades between the 1880s and 1920s, augmented by a relatively sparse inflow during the 1930s (when Canadian immigration policy virtually closed the doors) and a final surge of post World War II refugees. Small numbers of Yiddish writers were to be found among these settlers, some with reputations already established, others as aspiring novices, and for a time their poetry, fiction and drama furnished vivid connections with the world they had left, sustaining a fervent attachment to the landscape of their youth which they would never see again. For decades the immigrant community provided the Yiddish writer with a receptive audience, offering numerous publications for their works and, characteristically, sponsoring popular lecture series and public readings where creative writing and critical evaluations were presented and passionately discussed. However, this close-knit relationship between writer and audience was shared only by the first generation for whom Yiddish remained a richly expressive vernacular. For, like all other ethnic languages in Canada, Yiddish did not survive the acculturation of the immigrants' children and never succeeded in becoming their living language. Nor did any children of immigrants, seeking to become writers in Canada, ever adopt Yiddish as a means of expression.

The literary environment of these Yiddish writers fostered an emphatic reliance on evocative stores of memory but rendered depictions of the immediate present anxious and uncertain. Products of a traditional culture, they remained bound to the remembered Old World — claiming it "their home" even after decades of Canadian resettlement — deriving from it their diction, metaphors, and associations. These re-echoed ancient motifs as well as accounts of shtetl society which persisted in their imaginations long after its social existence had disappeared. Doubtless, it was the tragic destruction of their European birthplaces which impelled the writers to an unsurpassed fidelity to those hallowed memories. And their loyalty to the past must have resulted, in part, from their frustrations with a new cultural milieu which could not accommodate their language, cutting them off from the Canadian-born generations.

The result has been a distinctive body of literature, much of it written after many years of Canadian experience, which addresses obliquely, if at all, the new reality. It was as if these writers had not only spent their early years in European towns and villages, but that the memory of those disappeared worlds remained the most congenial region of their mature imaginations, indelible to their senses, shaping all their subsequent writing into a hauntingly eloquent chapter of the literature of exile.

When Yaacov Zipper arrived in Canada at the age of twenty-six from his native Poland, he was committed to the professional role of pedagogue, having recognized in the Jewish teacher an essential instrument in the process of national renewal made necessary by the upheaval of migration. Within a short time he embarked on the career of teacher and educational administrator in the Jewish Peretz Schools of Winnipeg and Montreal with which he was identified throughout his life and which gained for him the reputation as a leading figure in Jewish education in North America. For nearly five decades he was immersed in public affairs, deeply involved in the cultural life of the community, tirelessly engaged in moulding institutions capable of transmitting the knowledge and sympathetic understanding of the traditional Hebrew and Yiddish texts to generations of immigrant children confronting the prospect of assimilation in the surrounding culture.

Yet during all those years of active public life, Zipper's

deepest attachment was to the private act of writing. His daily immersion in educational and community affairs was a public role performed out of profound attachment to the life of his people. But his true vocation was the devotion to literature, which he pursued amidst the heavy demands of a crowded life, filling all his private hours with concentrated work of his own imagining. In the early morning hours before the household awakened, or late at night following exhausting meetings, and especially during the precious vacation months which he spent with his family in the Laurentian's Val David, he followed his imaginative life, seeking to capture in the story-teller's art a lasting vision of his rapidly changing world.

From the vantage point of his new home in Canada he looked back on the world of his origins, the pre-modern shtetl society created by East-European Jewry over the course of a millenium and conforming, in Zipper's particular case, to the ethos of Chassidic myth and mysticism. Shtetl life was relatively self-contained, practically isolated from the surrounding religions and cultures. It was a society organized to fulfill the intense religious strivings of the pious who conceived of worldly history as merely a transient moment anticipating the desperately awaited Messianic deliverance. Their desperation aptly reflected the powerless political and economic condition of shtetl Jews who, in their long history, had suffered the recurrent outrages visited upon them by the majority peoples with whom they lived and who, in consequence, came to envision themselves as selected for a spiritually powerful role in divine history.

By the late nineteenth century, however, the winds of social and political change had penetrated even the most remote of Jewish settlements in the Pale introducing the ideas of the Enlightenment some centuries after their revolutionary effect in western Europe, and, in particular, the disturbing modern concepts of rationalism, secularism, and radical social analysis. Yaacov Zipper was deeply affected by the new philosophy. While he had been raised in a traditional home and imbued by his father with a pious attitude and ready knowledge of the liturgy, sacred texts, and vivid folklore, he early enlisted in the modern struggle for the internal reorganization of shtetl society. His personal rebellion against the intellectual restrictions of traditional belief was expressed in his role as teacher, not in the orthodox cheder or yeshiva, but in the recently-fashioned secular mode which sought to give the student an awareness of the political and scientific world beyond the confines of the ghetto and, especially, to instill a sense of national dignity and personal assertiveness through the potent force of Socialist-Zionism.

For Zipper and his generation of Yiddish writers, the traditional Jewish world they had witnessed in their formative years was a world being torn asunder in the travail of conflicting ideologies, forcing often cruel choices upon its young between loyalty to the archaic unified past or to a future which would join Jewish fate to the rigorous history of modern Europe. In seeking to extend the boundaries of Jewish awareness beyond self-enclosed traditionalism, Zipper was formulating a response to the stultifying social and economic conditions of the shtetl. His deepest commitment was to the ineradicable humane spirit of shtetl life, but perceiving it weakened and enervated, he wished to strengthen it by fusion with the tougher modern notions of politics, psychology and cultural nationalism. Increasingly, the moral vitality of shtetl existence came to embody his ideal of exemplary conduct. In its simple piety, its studied unworldliness, its rapt concentration on the transcendental, he saw realized the secular ideals he pursued. Ironically, the further removed he was in time and place from his native scenes, the more was he drawn to them. He came to acknowledge that his quest for principles of individual and national fulfillment had been immanent in the lost mystical-religious stirrings of his childhood.

These dual elements — the avowedly secular outlook fused to the inherited metaphysical system — result in the tensions that animate Zipper's writing. In secularism he discovered the modern impulse — charted by Proust and Joyce — in which the autobiographical materials of personal history are endowed with universal significance. He saw his own life as the representative story of a whole generation in transition, uprooted and displaced from a familiar world which had become too cramped to satisfy the youthful appetite for experience, too narrow to sustain the modern soul's contradictory yearning for autonomy and engagement. But the twentieth century was hardly a propitious time for these youthful aspirations. The betrayal of the Soviet Revolution, the unleashed destructiveness of Nazism, the world's indifference to the murder of Europe's Jews — all served to undermine the Jewish intellectuals' faith in tolerance, sympathy and learning, values which Zipper had conceived as a bulwark against the approaching darkness. Under the duress of contemporary history, he did not abandon these ethical precepts, but rather reabsorbed them into the earlier primary values of "Yiddishkeit," a single term denoting the humane features of a morally sensitive Jewish conduct.

Zipper's fiction exemplifies the imaginative power that results from the tension between these components. Typically, his narrative method relies on an omniscient voice which bears the marks of a shtetl upbringing — deeply acquainted with its folklore, knowledgeable of its arcane Kabbalistic lore — but which now views it across the gulf of spiritual and geographical distance. Time has intervened, all is changed. Only the narrator's consciousness retains the semblance of that vanished place. Living in his mind, the past persists in the present, a source of light and warmth in a bleak world.

Memory alone, however, is too fragile a medium for the sacred aura of the past. Ultimately, only the redeeming powers of art protect against the corrosive inroads of loss and despair. Zipper has recourse to the niggun — the wordless melodies of Chassidism — as his symbol for the efficacy of the artistic process.

He conceives the singer of the niggun to be a celebrant who discovers in song the fullest expression of union with the ineffable, who wordlessly describes the unseen bond between man and God, who captures the human joy in natural existence without dispelling its inherent mystery. And by a slight extension of the metaphor, the singer of wordless refrains becomes the story-teller who fashions a permanent verbal image from the remembered life, thus retrieving it from the void. Art is a continuous niggun, the saving grace that alone can interpose between the life-that-was and the life-to-come. In the story-teller's reconstructions, our consciousness of a receding past achieves the permanent form which alone stays its dissolution — and our spiritual impoverishment.

Out of the fragmented shards of traditional Jewish life, Yaacov Zipper, by act of will and deep loyalty, imagined, then made real a home for his alien spirit. That this home consisted of a world of words attested both to the intensity of his exilic solitude and to his yearning for continuities. In the word — as in the niggun — he found the means for expressing his identity with the multitude of texts that had preceeded him and which affirmed Israel's historical persistence; at the same time such words — as in the wordless melody — became a current that bore the spirit of the exiled writer home at last.

Mervin Butovsky

GLOSSARY OF YIDDISH & HEBREW TERMS

apikoras	*heretic*
Baal Shem Tov	*18th century mystic, founder of Chassidism*
Bar Mitzva	*confirmation of Jewish male*
Beis Medrash	*house of study* *Bet Hamidrash (Hebrew)*
Chanukah	*holiday commemorating Maccabean victory*
chassid	*pious believer, member of community founded by Reb Israel Baal Shem Tov*
chaverim	*comrades, friends*
churb'n	*destruction resulting from attacks on Jewish communities*
dreidl	*spinning top*
gelt	*money*
goyim	*gentiles*
hakofah	*ceremonial procession during Simchas Torah* *hakofos (pl.)*
kaputta	*long, black coat worn by the pious*
kehilla	*community*
kri'shma	*daily prayer which states Judaic creed: "Hear, O Israel, the Lord is our God, the Lord is One."*
latutnik	*mender of clothing*
mikveh	*community ritual bath*

minyan	*a quorum of ten males required for communal religious services*
niggun	*wordless melody of Chassidim*
parnass	*leading official of synagogue*
rebbe	*Rabbi*
reb	*mister*
shabbos	*Sabbath*
shalom aleichem	*greeting, salutation*
shammes	*sexton or beadle*
sheitel	*wig worn by orthodox females*
shlimazl	*luckless character*
shochet	*ritual slaughterer*
shofar	*ram's horn used in religious ceremony*
shtetl	*Jewish village in Eastern Europe shtetlach (pl.)*
shul	*synagogue*
Simchas Torah	*holiday marking the completion of reading of the Torah*
Succos	*feast of the Tabernacles, a harvest festival*
t'hillim	*Psalms*
Tisha B'Av	*commemoration of the destruction of the Temple*
zaide	*grandfather*

BIOGRAPHICAL NOTE

Yaacov Zipper was born in the Polish town of Shebreshin in 1900. He was raised and educated in Tyszowce (Tishevitz), where his father Rabbi Avrohom Shtern, author of commentaries on the Talmud, post-Talmudic writings, and Chassidic parables, served as shochet (ritual slaughterer) and dayan (member of Rabbinical court).

Following an intensive Chassidic education in the traditional cheder, Zipper became committed to the secularist philosophy of Yiddish culture and trained as a teacher and youth educator, living and teaching in the towns of Ustilla and Ludmir, by the River Bug.

In November 1925, he emigrated to Canada where he took up the teaching post at the Yiddish secularist Jewish Peretz Schools, becoming principal in 1928. From 1930 to 1934 he occupied that post at a similar institution in Winnipeg, but reassumed his Montreal position in 1934, and until his retirement in 1971, was instrumental in creating one of the notable educational institutions in the community.

Throughout these years he was an important figure in Canadian Jewish literary affairs and played a leadership role in the Jewish Public Library, the Poalei Zion, the Jewish National Writers' Alliance, the Jewish Writers' Association, and in the Cultural activities of the Canadian Jewish Congress.

Zipper made his literary debut in 1923 with a short story about Chassidic life. His practice was to write a Yiddish version, to be followed by a Hebrew version. In addition to his stories and novels, Zipper edited a number of books, including the *Canadian Jewish Anthology* (with Chaim Spilberg), 1983, which received the National Jewish Book Award for that year. The recognition of his standing by international Yiddish-speaking audiences culminated in the award of the Manger

Prize for Yiddish Literature presented by the President of the State of Israel in 1982. Yaacov Zipper died in Montreal in April, 1983.

BIBLIOGRAPHY

Yaacov Zipper's publications appeared in Yiddish and Hebrew, the languages in which they were written. It was his custom to write the Yiddish version first to be followed, often many years later, by the Hebrew.

Books in Yiddish and Hebrew

Geven iz a Mentsch, Montreal, 1940.
Ish Hayah Ba'Aretz, Tel Aviv, 1955.

> *(There Was a Man*
> *Five stories based on the life of Rabbi Yisroel Baal Shem Tov,*
> *the founder of Chassidism.)*

Oif Yener Zeit Bug, Montreal, 1946.
Me'ever Lanahar Bug, Tel Aviv, 1957.

> *(On the Far Side of the River Bug*
> *A novel)*

Tzvishn Teichn un Vasern, Montreal, 1961.
Bein Naharot u'Nechalim, Tel Aviv, 1967.

> *(Amidst Rivers and Waters*
> *A biographical novel about shtetl life.)*

Ch'bin Vider in Mein Chorever Heim Gekumen, Montreal, 1965.

> *(I have returned once more to my destroyed home*
> *A poem on the Holocaust.)*

In Die Getzelten fun Avrohom, Montreal, 1971.
B'Ohelei Avraham, Tel Aviv, 1974.

> *(In the Tents of Abraham*
> *Narratives on biblical figures.)*

Fun Nechtn un Haint, Montreal, 1978.

> *(From Yesterday and Today*
> *A collection of stories and a journal of a visit to Israel.)*

Areinblicken in Yiddishen Literarishen Schaffen, Montreal, 1983.

> *(Glimpses into Yiddish Literary Creativity*
> *A collection of literary essays and profiles.)*

Books Edited

Jubilee Book of I.L. Peretz School, Winnipeg, 1934.
Jubilee Book of Jewish Peretz Schools, Montreal, 1938.
The Leizer Zuker Book, Montreal, 1968.
Pinkas Tishevitz, Tel Aviv, 1970.
Canadian Jewish Anthology (edited with Chaim Spilberg), Montreal, 1983.

Literary Awards

"Zukunft" Literary Prize for "Die Magefeh" (The Plague), 1942.
J. Friedland Award for "Dos Emese Bild" (The True Image), 1961.
J.I. Segal Award for Yiddish Literature, Montreal, 1974.
Ganopolsky Prize, Paris, 1979.
Manger Prize for Yiddish Literature, Israel, 1982.
Jewish Book Award for Yiddish Literature, New York, 1983.

ACKNOWLEDGEMENTS

The text of the dedication is from *Geven iz a Mentsch*.

"The True Image," "Light in the Darkness," "They Called Him Hunya," and "That First Morning" appeared in *Fun Nechtn un Haint*. "When the Lord was Angry" is from *In Die Getzelten fun Avrohom*; "Grebliya Street" is from *Tzvishn Teichn un Vasern*; "There was a Man" is from *Geven iz a Mentsch* and "At Home Again" is taken from the introduction to that work.

All the stories, with the exception of "The True Image" were translated by Ode Garfinkle and Mervin Butovsky. The English translation of "The True Image" by Sacvan Bercovitch first appeared in "Prism International" vol. 12, no. 3; "Light in the Darkness" was first published in English translation in "Writ 14," 1982.

The Huberman Foundation for Yiddish Culture provided support for publication. The translators are indebted to Sorke Zipper for her assistance and constant interest.